Carrie must have dozed, for the next thing she knew, the young patrolman was bending over her.

"Miss, would you come back to the desk?"

"Yes, certainly."

Sleepily she rose and followed him, stopping dead in her tracks as she rounded the corner. Matt Braden was standing in front of the captain's desk. She shuddered as she noticed the tense set to his jaw.

Matt's eyes flicked over her coldly. "Yes, she's my tenant," he said brusquely to the captain. "I'll take responsibility for her." He signed a sheet presented to him, and then turned to her. "Coming, Miss Craig?" he asked in a deceptively polite voice, but Carrie heard the undertone of anger, and stood uncertainly.

"I—I really don't think . . ." she began, but Matt strode to her side and took her arm in his iron grasp.

"Walk," he commanded in a fierce whisper, guiding her toward the front door.

LANGUAGE
OF THE
HEART

Jeanne Anders

Serenade/Serenata
BOOKS
of the Zondervan Publishing House
Grand Rapids, Michigan

A Note From the Author
I love to hear from my readers! You may correspond with me by writing:

> Jeanne Anders
> 1415 Lake Drive, S.E.
> Grand Rapids, MI 49506

LANGUAGE OF THE HEART
Copyright © 1985 by The Zondervan Corporation
1415 Lake Drive, S.E.
Grand Rapids, Michigan 49506

ISBN 0-310-46922-8

Edited by Ann McMath
Designed by Kim Koning

Printed in the United States of America

85 86 87 88 89 90 91 / 10 9 8 7 6 5 4 3 2 1

CHAPTER 1

CARRIE SLOWED THE BATTERED station wagon, pulled it off the highway onto the shoulder, and reached again for the crumpled road map. Pushing the tangle of long white-blond hair away from her face, she studied her route again, frowning in concentration. According to what the realtor had told her, the garage apartment should be located a few miles ahead.

"I'll take the next turn-off," Carrie decided aloud with a confidence she didn't really feel. "If only there wasn't so much traffic. I wonder if I'll ever get used to it?"

Life spent in a small town in southern Illinois had never prepared Carrie for the congestion, speed, and confusion of Chicago-area highways. She had learned to drive, like all members of her high school class, on quiet country roads. Her greatest challenge during her license test has been to parallel-park. How Gramps had grinned with glee when she described how she had almost bumped the instructor's car while maneuvering into the tiny space, only to discover later that the area would have held at least two pick-up trucks!

Carrie sighed, still hearing the echo of Gramps' laugh. But he was dead now, and with him had gone the only security she had ever known. That is, unless she could somehow find her sister, Beth. *Oh, Lord. I know she must be here in Chicago—somewhere. Please help me know where to start looking.*

Resolutely she squared her shoulders, flinging off the fine film of depression that threatened to settle around her again. A quick glance in her rear-view mirror showed a sports car approaching in her lane; she gauged that there was plenty of time before it caught up to her. She pressed the accelerator and the station wagon, rickety and sluggish, inched onto the highway, gradually picking up speed.

"Look out!" Carrie shouted as the red sports car, traveling faster than she had realized, gained on her much too quickly. In panic she swerved to the left lane, just as the sports car also swerved left. Carrie felt a sickening thud against her rear fender, and watched as the low-slung vehicle careened wildly around to her right, skidded, and came to a jolting stop.

"How dare he!" Carrie stormed indignantly, as she pulled her car onto the shoulder ahead of him. "He shouldn't be allowed on the road." But in the next breath she caught hold of her wildly careening thoughts. *I'm sorry, Lord. There goes my temper again.*

Carrie reached for the handle but before she could open it, the door was nearly wrenched off its hinges. A large hand reached into the car, encircled her wrist, and pulled her roughly to her feet.

"You little fool," the man shouted at her. "Where did you get a driver's license? Do you realize you could have killed me?"

"I could have killed *you* ?" Carrie's prayer was forgotten. "You were driving way over the speed limit, and—"

"And you poked onto the highway, and switched lanes without signaling," he interrupted. His eyes, an odd shade of gray—almost silver—held an expression that suddenly frightened her.

"Let go of me," she demanded, trying to pull away from his iron grip, but she was no match for his strength.

"When I'm good and ready," he muttered, leaning to look at the sticker on her windshield. "Downstate Illinois. I might have known. A country yokel, trying to drive in a big city—and doing a stupid job of it."

"I am not a yokel." Angry, she broke free from his hold just as she glimpsed a state police car gliding over the gravel, and stopping just inches away.

"Trouble, Miss?" the trooper asked, getting out of his car.

The promise of satisfaction helped her regain her composure. "Yes, Officer," she replied. "This man crashed into my car, and now he's threatening me."

With a glare at her, the other driver turned calmly to the trooper. "We seem to disagree on the cause of the accident," he said agreeably, all traces of his anger apparently gone.

Carrie stared in amazement as he spoke. *He could be conducting a board meeting,* she thought, stunned at his calm manner.

As the officer questioned him, she had a chance to size up this perplexing and thoroughly disagreeable person. She had to admit that he was handsome, perhaps the best-looking man she had ever seen, but that didn't lessen her instant dislike of him. About thirty years old, he was large, taller than she had first realized, with broad shoulders and a chest that seemed to strain his tan sweater to its very seams. The light tan corduroys were faded and worn, yet there was an air of sophistication about him. His hair was coal black, his face and hands deeply tanned despite the mid-April coolness, but it was his eyes—those piercing gray eyes occasionally flicking her way—that made her legs suddenly feel weak, as if she had no control over them. It was fear she felt. Those eyes seemed capable of anything.

She realized that the policeman was speaking to her. "Oh, I'm sorry," she apologized. "You were saying . . . ?"

"I asked if you had been injured," the trooper inquired. "You look pale."

"Oh, I'm fine, really," she assured him, ignoring the trembling that had suddenly begun in her knees. It was only after-shock, she told herself firmly, a natural reaction to the crash. Not for the world would she tell this trooper, especially with that horrible man looking on, that she had not eaten since yesterday, and that her fatigue, hunger, and grief were probably responsible for the deep shadows under her eyes. "I'm fine," she repeated, her hackles rising against the glint in the driver's eyes. "At least I *was* fine until he came along and ruined my car."

The trooper glanced at her battered wagon with wry amusement. "It looks like it's got its share of dents already,' he replied. "It's the other car that seems to be ruined."

She started to argue, and then looked for the first time at the low-slung red car.

It was a sleek, Mercedes-Benz convertible, she realized, and its left door was completely crumpled. Whatever sort of old clothes he wore, this stranger had to have a lot of money invested in a car like that. He was fortunate to have escaped serious injury.

The stranger's eyes were staring straight through her. "Your insurance card." He held out his own card curtly, and Carrie took a step back as she fumbled in her purse.

After a few more questions, the trooper summed up his accident report. "I'll have to give each of you a ticket." He began writing on his pad. "You, sir, for causing a rear-end collision, and you, miss, for hazardous entry on a freeway." He tore off the tickets, handed one to her, and smiled encouragingly. "You'll need a little practice before you can handle these roads. I strongly suggest that you get it."

He headed back to his car, and Carrie felt a stab of fear at being alone again with her accuser.

But there was no need to worry. He thrust her insurance card back at her, and gave her one more disgusted glance. Then he turned, and with an athlete's grace surprising in a man so large, swung himself over the side of the convertible, revved the engine, and skidded away, leaving bits of gravel whirling in his wake. Exhausted and drained, Carrie opened her car door and slumped into the front seat.

"Men!" she sighed, half-exasperated, half-disgusted, watching as the sun gently lowered into the clear horizon. Maybe the accident had been her fault; maybe she did need practice on city highways. But she had crossed the entire state of Illinois this week without mishap, and she had navigated countless Chicago highways too, looking for an apartment she could afford. And that was no small feat for a nineteen-year-old girl as sheltered and inexperienced as she.

And she had done it despite the grief in her heart, the overwhelming sense of loss that threatened constantly to engulf her in an agony of tears. She was proud that she hadn't wept since Gramps' death, proud of the way she had been able to attend to the funeral, hold her head up and handle things maturely as Gramps would have wished. He had given her this fierce sense of independence—along with a stubborn streak as wide as Kansas—and she knew he would be in death, as he had been in life, extremely proud of her.

But it was a bittersweet feeling, this sense of accomplishment. For in order to gain it, she had lost the one person she could depend on, the only human being who really loved her. If only she had phoned the doctor just a bit sooner, perhaps Gramps would still be alive . . . .

No. She shook her head firmly. Her grandfather had been lovable but stubborn, unwilling to hold still under any physician's probing examination.

"Just a touch of bronchitis," he had brushed aside her repeated questions, refusing to seek any medical aid. And after graduation, when her growing instinct told her that it was something more serious than bronchitis, and that she should put aside her plans to enroll at Illinois State University's art department, it was Gramps who raised the roof.

"No granddaughter of mine is going to waste her talents looking after me!" he had roared. "You pack up and get on to that school, girl, before I tan your hide."

But she had stood up to him. "I'm not a child anymore, Gramps," she had pointed out firmly, "and I can choose my own school. The junior college here will do nicely."

"Not on your life," Gramps grumbled, but he had eventually given in. Already in a weakened condition, he was closer to death than Carrie had realized, and not strong enough to overpower her this time.

And it had been the right decision. She wouldn't have traded those last cozy evenings when, after completing her homework, she would reach for her beloved craft materials and work on a piece of driftwood or a wooden plaque or perhaps just sketch in the warm, worn living room, for all the diplomas in the world.

"How I love to watch those deft fingers of yours, Carrie, my girl," Gramps would say, a touch of tenderness stealing into his hoarse voice.

And she would smile, covering her own sadness, and continue the nightly ritual. "A cup of tea, Gramps—to sleep on?"

Uncharacteristically, Gramps had even begun to discuss her parents, the couple who had been up until then only a shadowy recollection buried somewhere in the back of Carrie's mind. Now she came to know them as real people—the beloved red-head who was her mother, the tall blond, Gramps' son, who had taken this young widow and her daughter Beth, and made a home for them. And then Carrie had been born, binding the family together as one, never to be fragments again.

Only it hadn't worked out like that. For when she

was just four years old, her parents had been killed in an automobile accident, and her treasured half-sister Beth had vanished without a trace, a few days after the funeral.

"But why did she go, Gramps?" Carried had asked during one of those last intimate evenings. "I've always wondered, but you never wanted to talk about it. She was only sixteen at the time. Didn't she even leave a note?"

"A brief sort of scribble," Gramps had explained. "Said her reasons were too hard to talk about, but it was best that she was getting out of our lives. She reminded me that she was, after all, no kin of mine—"

"But she was *mine*—my only other relative!" Carrie had argued, feeling once again the remote misery, the bewildered feeling of abandonment that always stole over her whenever she thought of Beth. "Why did she leave us? And why didn't she ever write?"

"Well, she did write a few times . . . ."

"Gramps! You never told me."

"Didn't want to get your hopes up." Gramps had reached for his pipe. "I knew you was pining away, storing up hurt in your little-girl heart, wondering why everyone you had ever loved had to go away and leave you . . . ."

Touched, she had reached impulsively for his hand. "I had you, Gramps," she reminded him softly.

"That you did," he harrumphed. And to hide his tender feelings he had gone to the old corner desk and pulled out a yellowed envelope. "I got this four years ago," he had told Carrie, handing the letter to her. "There's been nothing since."

Carried pulled herself out of her reverie. Fatigue

had almost overtaken her, and if she didn't get moving along the highway soon, it would be nightfall.

"And if there's anything I hate more than driving during the day," she reminded herself wryly, "it's driving at night."

She guided the car onto the pavement, taking extreme care to check in all directions for on-coming traffic and assuring herself that the dark-haired stranger was miles away by now. She was relieved when the station wagon surged ahead with a surprising burst of power.

It was no use dwelling on Gramps, she told herself firmly, or thinking about Beth either, at least until she had herself settled. Her most important task right now was to locate and, she hoped, rent the garage apartment the realtor had told her about that afternoon. At least then she would have shelter for the night, and a base from which to start her search for a job and for her half-sister.

The freeway exit was just ahead and Carrie guided the car over the ramp and onto a two-lane road that seemed surprisingly rural after the heavy traffic she had just left behind. Despite her weariness she found herself intrigued by the small roadside mailboxes that popped into view every half-mile or so. The setting was country-like, too: soft, rolling hills, an occasional barn in the distance, paths leading from the road into wooded areas that obscured the view of large old farmhouses and estates.

It's just like home, Carrie thought, feeling almost comfortable for the first time since her tiring journey had begun. It was hard for her to believe that this beautiful setting was so close to a large, bustling city like Chicago.

She almost missed her turn—but no, there it was on the old mailbox: Pine Tree Lane, Matthew Braden, Prop. She turned gratefully into the long driveway. Matthew Braden was the owner of the property, the real estate agent had explained. He had purchased it last fall, had begun immediately to make improvements, and the garage apartment had only been listed that afternoon.

"He hasn't even decided on the rent yet," the realtor had warned her, "so the place may still be a bit shabby." But Carrie didn't care. She had never had many material possessions. And hadn't Gramps always said that God would take care of their needs?

She wondered if her fierce sense of independence had grown since Gramps' death. God might take care of her needs, but certainly she would have to make her own way in the world. If the Lord wanted to give her a shove now and then in the right direction, then that was His prerogative, but mostly she felt it was up to her. She felt proud of the inner strength her stand required, and if it also meant an infuriating temper that got in the way of her show of independence, well then, so be it . . . . But just as often Carrie secretly felt incapable of changing herself. If she couldn't even control her temper, how could she mold herself into the person—the calm, assured, independent woman who knew her own mind and acted on it—that she wanted to be? She would pray about it, and continue to ask God to help her change, but ultimately, she felt it was up to her to grow stronger, to wash away doubts about her own adequacy.

Carrie lifted her hand to her temple as another wave of fatigue moved over her. She found herself hoping desperately that Mr. Matthew Braden had not yet rented his apartment, for she was exhausted.

The property, although somewhat overgrown, did not look a bit shabby. As she wound the car slowly around the road's narrow turns, Carrie found her heart lifting at the sight of the stately pines that did indeed line the lanes. There were elms and maples too, still drooping with traces of late winter, but bearing new green buds as well. What a perfect picture the landscape would make in just a week or two when spring burst forth in all of its abundance. Carrie caught sight of purple and yellow crocuses peeking from the sodden earth, and within the depths of her being, she responded. Maybe God was looking out for her small needs as well as her big ones.

"I've come home, little crocuses," she whispered, feeling light-headed and a little silly. "I'll pick you and put you in a beautiful yellow dish in my new apartment, and you will make me happy every time I look at you."

Swinging the station wagon past the last turn, she stopped in the middle of a paved courtyard that looked out across a field. To her left was a massive stone house, solid and reassuring, looking as if it had stood there forever. A distance behind it, almost lost in the lengthening shadows, was a smaller structure, possibly the garage she was seeking. The deepening sunset bathed both buildings in a rosy glow coloring them a warm and inviting pink. Carrie sighed, savoring the view.

No matter *what* the condition of the garage apartment, she knew she had to have it. The countryside, the relaxed and peaceful surroundings, had already restored her spirits as nothing else had been able to during these last painful weeks. Here she would find solitude, peace, the strength to do what she had to do. Hurriedly, she swung her legs out of the car.

17

"Hi!" said a small shy voice, and Carrie looked down in surprise. A little dark-haired boy, wearing a jean jacket, denims, and cowboy boots stood before her, light eyes wary yet curious.

"Well, hello," she smiled, and laid a welcoming hand on his shoulder. He allowed her to do so, continuing his grave scrutiny, eyes peeping through the thick fringe of black bangs.

"Are you going to live in the garage?" he asked finally.

"I hope so," she told him, and was rewarded by a smile of such sweetness that her heart instantly warmed. "Would you like to look at it with me?"

"I've already seen it, but I'll show you around."

She smiled, grasping his outstretched hand, and turned down the path with him.

The child's name was Michael, he told Carrie as they strolled along. He was seven years old and he lived, he explained vaguely, "over there." Beyond those tidbits of information, however, he would not go. Carrie sensed a reticence in him, a guarded almost nervous disposition that would not let him feel at ease with a stranger. She was glad for his company however, and knew somehow that he was equally grateful for hers, despite the absence of easy chatter that most children bestowed upon her. And when she reached the garage, she was doubly glad that Michael was there to share her pleasure.

"Why, Michael, it's beautiful!" she said, gazing at the strong stone walls.

"It needs flowers." He frowned at the barren earth rimming the small building.

"Of course. But we'll plant those right away now that the weather is warming."

18

"We will?"

"Definitely." She closed her eyes, seeing the beauty. "Astors and marigolds to set off the yellow in the brick. And pansies, too. You'll like their funny little faces!"

He smiled again, that rare sweet expression and then pulled open the huge double doors. She stepped inside as he flicked on the light switch, pleased that the electricity was hooked up, for the sun was nearly gone now.

"Why, it really *is* a garage," she mused doubtfully, looking at the concrete floor recently swept clean. "It's big, but I wonder . . . ."

"This isn't the apartment, this is where you put your car," Michael told her seriously, and turned to a flight of stairs running up the inside of the wall. "It's the upstairs that's being fixed."

"Of course," she smiled, relieved. "My ignorance is showing."

"What's ignorance?"

"Something that you don't have to worry about, my smart friend," she teased, and followed him up the stairs. Once again he turned on the light and Carrie blinked, awed.

An empty but massive room awaited her view, its floor newly covered by a layer of gleaming dark wood. Carrie inhaled the aroma of the hardwood. Its rich color set off the small fireplace on the far wall, and picked up the hues of the sunset glowing through a deep bay window. The entire room seemed washed in gold and she suddenly realized why. "Oh, Michael," she breathed. "Look, there's a skylight."

Michael shrugged. "It's all right, I guess."

"All right! It's the best thing that could have

happened. A skylight will give me the most glorious natural light for my work. I'm an artist of sorts." She moved over to the bay window under which a waist-length set of shelves, still unvarnished, ran its entire length. "A perfect place to work, looking out onto the fields . . ."

To her left was a small kitchenette, behind it a bath, still unenclosed. But, no matter—it was all meant for her and she would have it if it took her last dime. She turned to the little boy. "Michael, thank you for showing this to me. It's absolutely perfect."

Michael studied her solemnly for a moment. "I like you," he said finally, bashfully, as if he were present-ing her with a bouquet. She sensed it had taken him courage to speak the words. "I like you a lot better than Aunt Barbara."

"Aunt Barbara?"

"Uh-huh," he nodded. "She smiles at me with her mouth, but you smile at me all over your face." And with that pronouncement he turned for the stairs. "It's getting dark, Carrie, and I'll be late for supper. So long."

"Michael, wait. Should I walk you home?" she asked, but his cowboy boots had already hit the cement floor below. She heard the slam of the garage door. Perhaps he could find his way alone. Somehow he seemed very much at home in this environment. But it was almost evening, and she realized with a start that she had better get back and hunt for Mr. Braden before anyone else viewed the apartment.

She hurried back along the darkened path, but wasn't at all fearful. She felt peaceful with the rustling wind around her, the tree boughs that swayed grace-fully, seemingly bending to her in a sort of comradeship. Hurriedly she came out into the driveway and stopped, noticing a gleam of light shining through the half-open front door of the house.

She walked up to it, straightened her shoulders, and knocked.

In a few moments she heard heavy footsteps approaching, and the door swung open. There before her disbelieving eyes stood a tall stranger in a crew-necked sweater and tan corduroys. But no, not a stranger.

"Well," he said, looking down at her, big and powerful. "So we meet again."

CHAPTER 2

"OH. NO!" CARRIE SAID. half-aloud. "You—you're not Matthew Braden, are you?" she asked, hoping feverishly that he was not. But the truth dawned on her as she vaguely remembered seeing his name on the insurance card after the accident. Why hadn't it registered sooner?

He answered gruffly. "Who did you think I might be, since you followed me out here? What is it you want?"

Carrie was speechless. He hardly looked like the lord and master of such an estate. But even though he resembled a rugged farm hand, his air of authority was unmistakable.

"And what are you staring at?"

"I . . . that is . . . you don't look like a landowner."

"And how are landowners supposed to look? Would you have us wear dinner jackets when we ride horses?"

"Horses? Really?" Carrie forgot her discomfort

momentarily. "Are there stables nearby? Do you have your own horse?" She hadn't even considered the possibility that if she lived here, she might have a chance to ride again, and the idea thrilled her.

Perhaps it was her genuine pleasure that thawed Matt slightly, for he answered her almost pleasantly. "I haven't purchased a horse yet, but there's a stallion that interests me. I was driving from the stables when we . . . met."

Carrie flushed, remembering the scene on the road. She wondered if he rode a horse the way he drove, with reckless abandon. Her thoughts must have been mirrored in her face, for he cast her a cool smile.

"And what is it I can do for you, Miss . . ."

"I'm Carolyn Craig," she told him, "and I want to rent your apartment."

He eyed her suspiciously for a few moments, then he opened the door fully, and turned and began walking, apparently expecting her to follow. She quickly stepped behind him through the foyer of immense proportions, gleaming with dark wood trim. Pale green wallpaper stretched to a twenty-foot ceiling where a huge chandelier cast a quiet glow. She could hear dogs barking in the distant recesses of the house. He turned left into a room that was undoubtedly his study, and sat down behind a desk, motioning for her to take the leather chair opposite him.

She felt uncomfortable—albeit determined—and waited for him to speak first. He obliged her almost immediately, but his question caught her off guard.

"You don't trust me, do you, Miss Craig?" He leaned back comfortably in his chair.

Carrie shifted uneasily; offending him would not help her cause, but he was an insufferable man. "No,

I suppose I don't trust you very much, Mr. Braden. You're probably a decent person, and granted, I have no right to judge, but all I've seen thus far is your anger. I find it . . . quite outrageous." There. Perhaps she had gone too far, but he had asked her, and it was not like Carrie to dodge a challenge.

"Well put." He studied her intently with just a trace of a genuine smile hovering around his lips. Was he actually pleased with her honesty—or with himself for projecting a certain appearance? Carrie wasn't sure. And then the gray eyes grew lighter as he leaned forward. "And if I'm so disagreeable," he asked her quietly, "why do you wish to rent property on my grounds?"

Carrie hesitated for a moment. This was a question she had not yet asked herself although she knew it was reasonable. Matt Braden actually frightened her, although she wouldn't admit it to him. His personality reminded her of a banked fire, ready to flare the minute it was exposed to air and a new supply of something to burn. And yet a very small part of her, the part that was an awakening woman, found him attractive, so magnetic that danger signals went off in her head.

What was even more disturbing was his altered attitude. The open hostility that he had earlier displayed was masked now, hidden behind a facade of politeness, but Carrie sensed that it was still present. She didn't understand why he was now making an effort at decency. He would not be an easy man to have living nearby, but perhaps if she simply stayed as far away from him as possible . . . And then there was the beauty of her surroundings to consider. How could she forgo this peaceful place? She leaned forward to answer his question, her eyes honest.

"I'd like to rent your apartment because it's in the middle of a world I need right now. Not only is the property beautiful, but the apartment itself—well, it's simply a miracle what has been done with it. The whole interior has a glow of beauty that reflects good taste and care and . . ."

She stopped and bit her lip. She wasn't telling him anything he didn't know! He was no doubt the one who had designed it. And her praise implied a friendliness she simply couldn't afford, not if she wanted him to keep his distance.

"You approve, it seems." He watched her carefully as she nodded her assent. "And you want the property quite a bit, don't you?"

She looked down at her purse, conscious of the barely-perceptible smile on his face. He was playing a game with her, mocking her, holding the apartment out as a prize to be snatched away at the proper moment. Carrie felt a flash of anger at her own humble dependence. But if he wanted her to beg, then that's what she would do. The prize was worth it.

Her thoughts were interrupted by the shrill ringing of the telephone and Matt's tanned hand caught it up.

"Yes?" he spoke into the receiver. "Yes, Operator, this is he." And a moment later, as Carrie watched in disbelief, he swung into a torrent of perfectly-accented French.

Was there no end to this man's versatility, she wondered? He rode horses, spoke French, and refurbished old homes with a degree of sensitivity that warmed her artistic heart. She glanced around his study, noticing that the pale green carpet looked like new. A pair of loveseats in the far corner were apparently being reupholstered, but from the swatch of material lying across an arm, Carrie guessed that the finished furniture would be in the best of taste. What would it be like to create—and live in—a home so lavish?

She turned back, watching him converse with the overseas caller, and noticed the genuine and charming smile on his handsome face, making him appear almost boyish. He and the caller were apparently good friends—Carrie's high school French was good enough to catch a few lines—and at one point, as he threw back his head and laughed easily, she found herself wishing that his whimsey had been directed at her. What would it be like to meet Matt's eyes and find humor there, instead of tension and menace?

He hung up suddenly, and swung around to open one of the desk drawers. "Sorry for the delay," he told her in a business-like manner, all traces of lightness now vanished. "That was a call from Paris I had been waiting for all evening."

"You speak French very well," she told him, unable to contain her admiration.

"I took a minor in languages in college," he answered carelessly. "It turned out to be good preparation for the imports business." He tossed a printed form onto the desk and reached for a pen. "All right," he sighed, "let's get this over with. Your name is Carolyn Craig," he scrawled it in a space, "and you are employed where?"

Her mouth dropped. Was he actually giving her the lease? Happiness swept through her, even sweeter because it had not been anticipated. "I'm not employed as yet, but I will be tomorrow. I'm getting a job at Woodfield."

"Woodfield? Good. It's only ten minutes from here.

You won't have a chance to kill too many people on the highway.'' Carrie tensed but she saw he was actually smiling. He went on quickly. ''The rent is, ah, one hundred sixty per month, not including utilities, and the first month is payable in advance.''

He swung the lease over to her and she signed quickly before he had a chance to change his mind. Then, taking the battered wallet out of her purse, she counted $160 out carefully and slid the bills across the desk. He had already written her a receipt and she stuffed it quickly into her purse.

''Oh, there's one more thing,'' he told her, rising from the desk and striding to the door of the study. ''Stay here for a moment, please.''

He disappeared down the hall and in a moment she heard his returning stride, along with the distinct clicking of paws along the smoothly waxed floor. Matt rounded the doorway, holding onto the collars of two incredibly handsome German Shepherds.

''Oh!'' Carrie sighed in stunned admiration of the dogs. ''They're absolutely beautiful!''

She moved toward them, but Matt's sharp voice stopped her, and she realized that each dog had his fangs bared, his head lowered. They had formed a protective barrier around Matt and were obviously planning to attack her should she move toward them. Carrie swallowed, and hastily backed away.

Commanding the dogs to stay, Matt took his hands from the their collars and walked past them to Carrie. Keeping his eyes on the dogs, he put one hard arm around her. Carrie looked up at him, surprised and flustered. The sensation of his nearness was surprisingly pleasant.

But it was obvious that he was not similarly

27

affected by her. He was offering this gesture for the dogs' sake as he watched them carefully, and finally spoke.

"This is Carolyn," he told the shepherds formally, as if she were being introduced to royalty. "She will be staying here. She is a friend."

He snapped his fingers and the dogs were instantly in motion, bounding toward Carrie with wagging tails and dangling tongues.

"Why, they're as playful as puppies!" she exclaimed. "Not at all the ferocious guard dogs they seemed just a minute ago." She buried her face in their thick fur and hugged them with no trace of fear.

"Oh, they're ferocious, all right," Matt commented, "when they're supposed to be. Their names are Mac and Tosh, and they roam the property at will when I'm not here. Now that they know you, you need have no fear—as a matter of fact you'll be quite safe out in the garage."

He turned to his desk with the same aloof attitude he had earlier shown her, and Carrie realized that their brief moment of pleasantness was over. "If there's nothing more, Miss Craig . . ."

"Just the keys, Mr. Braden," she matched his formal tone. "I'd like to move into the garage right away."

He looked up in surprise. "The apartment won't be ready for several days, Miss Craig. It's only the nineteenth of April, and your lease doesn't start until May first. Do you always sign things without reading them first?"

He was mocking her again, but her deep disappointment was the only emotion she could handle. "It doesn't matter, really, Mr. Braden," she pleaded. "I

28

don't care what shape the place is in. I'd sleep anywhere right now."

He leaned back in the chair, and the tight look again etched his jawline. "I'll see you in May, Miss Craig."

"Don't think that thought brings me any pleasure!" she hurled over her shoulder as she stamped from the room and slammed the front door loudly. The nerve of him!

But in spite of her fury as she walked across the driveway, Carrie could feel a bubble of triumph rising within her. She had the apartment! No matter that his change of heart had been somewhat suspicious; Matt Braden had decided to rent to her and she was absurdly grateful.

She sat in her car, considering her situation, uneasily aware that the advance rent payment had left her with only a few dollars in her purse. She had spent a tidy sum on gasoline this past week, and even if she did land a job tomorrow, there was no telling when she would be paid. So a motel, and a decent meal, and a soft bed and blessedly hot bath were beyond her reach at present.

Never mind. She would think of something. She could even find a shoulder on the road, someplace hidden by shrubbery, and sleep in her car. She had done it several times, and although it made her feel somewhat sordid, she would have to do it again. She eased the car down the driveway, and headed out onto the road, stopping a few miles down where a lake shimmered quietly in the moonlight.

Carrie got out of the car and moved stealthily toward the lake. Reaching down, she splashed the water onto her face and arms, shivering at the lake's icy tingle. She wished fervently that she could change into something more comfortable for sleeping than her jeans, but was grateful that she was at least dressed warmly. People did freeze in their cars; the deceptively gentle spring air of the midwest could turn bitter within moments and she had to be prepared.

Groping in the back of the station wagon, she laid out clothes for the morning, casting a wistful look at the boxes that held her small store of possessions. How she longed for a room of her own, where her beloved craft materials could be neatly stored, her clothes hung in orderly fashion. But it would all come in time. She had succeeded in her first objective, despite her arrogant landlord. And now she would go after the next.

Once back on the front seat of the station wagon, chewing an apple thoughtfully, Carrie remembered again how the soft dark hair had fallen across Matt's forehead, how he had smiled so engagingly into the telephone receiver. Then she shrugged and reached into the glove compartment for the yellowed letter that she had kept since the evening Gramps had shown it to her. It was dated four years ago, postmarked Chicago, and she read it again by the light of the small bulb although she knew every word.

Dear Gramps, her sister had written, *I am settled here in the big city, and life is good. I am working at a job I enjoy at one of the largest shopping malls in the world. Give Carrie a hug for me, and please don't worry. Love, Beth.*

Please don't worry, Beth had said. But even though Carrie had only a fleeting memory of the red-haired teenager Beth had once been, she *did* worry. Why had Beth left? Had she been in some sort of trouble? And why had she never returned? Once again the lost

30

feeling of loneliness swept across her, and Carrie swallowed hard against it.

Beth was her sole relative now, the only link with her past. She had to find her sister, and she would. Carrie closed her eyes while the unknown image of Woodfield danced before her. Woodfield: the world's largest indoor shopping mall . . .

CHAPTER 3

IT WAS HER FAVORITE TIME of the day when Carrie awoke—the soft early morning when the dew hung lavishly, turning trees and grass frosty in the pale glint of sunlight. But she stretched her stiff limbs and groaned in misery. Sleeping in an uncomfortable car had left her almost as tired and sore as she had been the night before. But gradually, as feeling returned to her aching legs, she felt more optimistic, and attempted to think of more pleasant subjects. Such as the possiblity of a job.

She had told Matt Braden last night that she was planning on working at Woodfield. The actual truth, however, was that she had only the local newspaper want ads, listing two jobs presently available, and her own natural optimism to back up her statement. But surely one of these two positions would become hers today. Her self-confidence was filling her face with smiles, although she knew at the same time that the odds she would find Beth were stacked against her.

There were numerous shopping malls in the Chicago area, and even though Woodfield was the largest, Carrie had no real certainty that Beth had ended up there. Or perhaps she had, and had moved on again, or changed her name through marriage. But, no matter. Somewhere in this metropolitan area of some seven million people, one or two had known Beth Anderson and would remember her. Woodfield was as logical a place as any to begin the search.

Resolutely, Carrie started her car and edged out onto the road. Before long she spotted a service station, pulled in, and slipped into the restroom to change her clothes. Once dressed, she eyed herself critically in the mirror. The rose-colored suit was a bit wrinkled, but fitted her small slim figure perfectly, for she had made it herself on the battered sewing machine that had been her mother's, and now reposed, ancient but workable, in the back of the car. Her hair—now there was a problem. Long, thick, and soft—how fortunate that she had washed it at the motel just the night before last—it had been appropriate on a college campus, but was too girlish for someone about to become a career woman. Shrugging, she reached for her purse and old clothes. However she looked, it was the best she could do for now.

The rush hour had already passed, making traffic light, and as Carrie sped along the highway she passed the place where yesterday's collision had taken place. Smoldering at the memory, her mind drifted back to Matt Braden. What a strange, challenging, absolutely *irritating* person! In a way he repelled her, and yet she knew instinctively that there was more to him than the rough exterior he had presented. She thought for a moment of the way his arm had felt around her shoulders—strong and firm—then pushed the memory from her mind. He had made it all too clear that she was an unwanted nuisance, so how could she feel any differently about him?

Finally she spotted Woodfield's red and gold dome, and sent up a prayer of relief as she navigated the mall's parking lot. Even though the center had just opened, the lots were jammed with cars and pedestrians.

"Is it always this busy?" she asked a woman alighting from a car in the next parking stall.

"This is nothing," the woman answered. "You ought to see it around Christmas time. Wall to wall people."

"Sure is impressive," Carrie remarked, remembering her hometown shopping area: three emporiums servicing a handful of people each day.

She walked to the outside door of a large department store, and wound her way inside to another door that lead into the mall. She stopped short at the sight.

High above the gleaming white walls, intriguing geometric cut-outs on the ceiling cast interesting light-patterns on a scene that Carrie would have described as a main street shopping district. Stores lined the mall, specializing in everything from gourmet food to jewelry, and sunken brick rest-stops were available everywhere with people lounging comfortably in the carpeted areas, eating ice cream and surveying the swiftly-moving crowds. Directly ahead of her rose a delicate metal sculpture, lifting its arcs in a graceful design, and as she followed it upward she saw that the mall was criss-crossed on all sides by second floor ramps above her head, moving yet another flow of traffic. Live greenery was everywhere and background music offered a peaceful touch.

Eyes rapt, she took the folded newspaper page from her purse, scanned the secretarial ad and the crafts store's ad and approached a man who appeared to be a security guard for directions.

Then armed with a folder of the floor plan of the three-storied mall, which he had given her, Carrie strolled toward the Grand Court. She would go to Wood and Plants first, she decided. Not only would the job there involve working with crafts, which interested her far more than a typing job, but it was closer, a decidedly important factor. She had the feeling that she could walk herself into exhaustion here if she weren't careful, and it would be embarrassing to faint with thousands of people looking on!

She reached what surely must be the Grand Court and stared in amazement. The mall had moved into three levels now, she noticed, and she watched as people moved easily from one floor to another. A stunning red and blue ceiling sculpture hung over the Court and there were fountains too, sparkling water bursting into small brick enclosures lined with benches. Carrie noticed shoppers strolling behind the waterfalls, and realized that the bricks were cut into tunnels.

In the center of the court, several children were gathered around a puppet theater, watching with pleasure as two marionettes portrayed the story of Punch and Judy. Carrie moved closer, and thought suddenly of Michael, the little boy she had met yesterday, and wondered if his mother or his Aunt Barbara (if that was with whom he lived) would allow her to take him to Woodfield someday. Perhaps he had been here many times, but she wished he were now at her side, appreciating the puppet show with her. Child-like pleasures were always more enjoyable if they were shared, especially with a little boy as sweet and shy as Michael.

She moved on now, conscious of her growing fatigue. She had to get these interviews out of the way quickly while she still had some energy left. Then she would have to see what she could do about getting a meal with the few dollars she had left. Turning right, she passed several stores and then saw the sign: Wood and Plants.

The interior of the store was filled with hanging baskets, small figurines, and framed prints, and her heart leaped in pleasure. This was the environment her artistic soul most appreciated. She took a deep breath and, walking into the store, spotted a tall, blond man writing busily at the counter.

"Hi!" she greeted him when he looked up. "I've come to see about the job."

With a glance he took in her small, delicate appearance, and a look of frank admiration spread across his attractive features. "And hello to you," he smiled back.

"Is it still open?" she asked quickly.

"The job? Yes, and if it wasn't," he said, coming around the counter, "I might fire whoever I just hired, and give it to you instead." For a moment his expression became serious. "Have you any experience?"

"I've done a lot of clerking in retail stores back home, and I was an art major in college . . . ."

"Enough said. You're hired." The grin was back and she looked at him with astonishment.

"Really? Seriously? That was the shortest job interview I've ever had!"

He put out his hand. "I'm Jason King, age twenty-six, five-foot-ten, 170 pounds, handsome, trustworthy, and owner of Wood and Plants. How about you?"

"That's a hard act to follow," she smiled, taken aback by his cheeriness, but enjoying the first kind words an adult had spoken to her in a long time. "I'm Carolyn Craig, but my friends call me Carrie."

"Then, Carrie, it is," he said, his eyes sweeping her again with open pleasure and finally resting on her left hand, where the absence of a ring told him what he obviously wanted to know. "Come on in back, Carrie, and we'll get down to business. Store business, that is."

She followed him, her mind whirling. Things were certainly happening quickly! And although she sensed that Jason would not be her usual choice of boyfriend—he was too bold, too assured of his own charm for her tastes—he seemed nice, and working with him would be quite an experience. She seated herself on a stool in the back of the cluttered shop, and listened carefully to his explanation.

Apparently there were two housewives who helped Jason in the store, each splitting a shift, but one of them had taken a recent leave of absence in order to have surgery.

"And with summer approaching," Jason explained, "she's thinking about quitting in order to be home during her children's vacation. Which leaves me in somewhat of a bind because business is improving, and I need a full-time worker to replace her."

"Oh, I can work full time," Carrie assured him. "In fact, I—I must."

"Supporting yourself?" he asked, and she nodded. "Well," Jason mused, "the salary here might not be enough for that." Carrie did some quick mental calculations with the figure he named.

"My rent's one hundred sixty. . . ." she thought aloud.

"One sixty! Boy, that's a real steal, especially around this area," Jason told her, and then a teasing look spread across his face. "Unless, of course, that's only your *half* of the rent."

Carrie blushed. "I'm not sharing my apartment with anyone, if that's what you mean," she reassured him with a trace of annoyance.

"Now, now . . ." He backed away in mock dismay. "I meant a female roommate, of course."

"I'll just bet you did!" she retorted, but couldn't help laughing. She had never known anyone quite so brash, and likeable at the same time. Some of the men she had dated had not wanted to give her the time of day once they realized she was not going to compromise beliefs they regarded as prudery. But she had a feeling that though Jason might be disappointed to learn of her standards for dating relationships, he would simply laugh and continue to be her friend.

She went back to her figuring, and decided that if she cut back on groceries, she could probably make all her expenses. "There will be raises, of course," he explained, and then launched into a discussion of her duties.

Woodfield was open from ten in the morning to ten at night, and she and Jason would take turns coming in early and staying late. The part-time employees would fill in the gaps, and she would work a few hours on Saturday as well.

38

"It's a perfect arrangement, Jason," she approved warmly.

He returned her smile, then perched casually on the edge of a stool. "Now, tell me about yourself, Carolyn Craig."

She hesitated. How much of her background was he entitled to know? Would it be wise to tell such an obvious playboy that she was all alone in the world? Instead she explained briefly about her search for her sister, making it sound as though she and Beth had a home waiting back in downstate Illinois.

"Beth Anderson?" he thought for a moment. "I haven't come across anyone by that name here . . . . And if you were planning to go through employees' records, that stuff is usually confidential." Then, noting her disappointment, he amended his words. "Just because I don't know Beth doesn't mean she isn't here, Carrie, or hasn't worked here in the past. There are thousands of employees at Woodfield, and I'm sure if you ask around the various stores, someone will remember her."

"I'll do that."

He leaned forward. "And besides coming from a little town, Carrie, what else should I know about you? What do you do for . . . ah . . . fun?"

She ignored his insinuation, and instead told him about her artwork. "I started making little crafts a few years ago," she explained. 'First terrariums, then glazed plaques, straw dolls, a bit of macrame. That's why I'm certain I'll enjoy working here. Your items are very much like the ones I make."

"Really?" There was interest in his eyes. "Do you have any samples with you?"

"Why, yes, I have several boxes in my station

wagon. At his puzzled glance, she added hastily, "I just haven't had time to unpack them yet." Jason was the last person who should know she was sleeping in her car each night.

"Do you think you could bring some in now?" Jason asked. "I might like to purchase them on consignment."

"Well . . . certainly." She rose, pleased at the idea. "I'll bring in a box right now."

"Drive your car around to this side of the mall," he advised with a grin. "Otherwise, you might turn into a grandmother before you find your way back, and I like you just the way you are."

Blushing furiously, she went out of the mall, remembering gratefully that she had parked her car under a #10 sign. This was the hugest place she had ever seen and, gratefully, she was now a part of it. She thought briefly of the Jiffy Type job, and wondered if it would have paid more; she was going to have a struggle keeping afloat financially. But she shrugged off the worry. If things got too rough, she could always add a part-time job to her schedule. She would figure something out.

After reparking the car and coming back through another entrance, Carrie noticed a store similar to Jason's called The Brass Ring. She stopped for a moment, surveying its displays, and decided that most of the merchandise was of superior quality to Jason's. Although she hadn't had much time to look, Wood and Plants had given her the impression of a rather inexpensive store, while this place sold some lovely antiques as well as imported pieces. She would come back again, and peruse the store more thoroughly when she had time. It would be a pleasure to view such stunning merchandise.

She reached Jason, and as she unloaded her box, she saw the alert gleam in his eyes, replaced almost immediately by a polite, almost off-hand expression.

"Very nice," he murmured casually, picking up a few pieces. "The terrariums are out of style now, of course, but I suppose we could stock a few. I'll put a small display table at the entrance, and we'll price everything at about six to eight dollars. You'll get half of the sale profit. What do you say?"

Carrie thought a moment. Her commission seemed quite small. The materials, of course, cost her practically nothing, since she could turn bits of scrap into little works of art, but each item took several hours to finish. Shouldn't her time be worth more than that?

But, of course Jason was the businessman, not she. She had never sold any of her work, never even thought of it until now, and he was offering her a chance at some much-needed extra income.

"That would be fine, Jason," she smiled.

"Good." She thought she noted a dark glow of satisfaction—and something else?—in his eyes. But once again he was his usual, casual self, and he motioned her back into the stockroom, and gave her forms to fill out.

"By the way," she told him as she scribbled her way through the papers, "I saw our competition on the way back."

"Oh, you mean The Brass Ring?" he asked. "It's quite a bit classier than this operation, but they cater to a wealthier clientele. *I* belong to the common man," he said grandly.

She chuckled. "Then I'll have to go back and see what the common man is missing."

"Do that. Their inventory is quite tasteful," he told

41

her seriously. "The Brass Ring is run by a husband-and-wife team, Liz and Larry Fields. They're a nice couple."

Carrie finished the forms, and Jason suggested that she have a bite to eat and return for a short stint of duty.

"Just to get acquainted with it all," he pointed out. "You can go home at four, and take the late shift tomorrow."

Carrie did as he suggested. The faintness that had been plaguing her all day had finally caught up to her, and she found an inexpensive restaurant as soon as she could. Savoring each pungent spoonful of meaty soup, she hoped fervently that its nutrition would hold her over for awhile. Jason had told her that she would not be paid for two weeks, and it was going to be quite a challenge to stretch her remaining cash into enough groceries and gasoline until then.

But throughout the remainder of the afternoon, as she conscientiously waited on customers, and felt the glow of Jason's approving smile, her spirits rose once again. It would all work out, she promised herself. And as soon as she was settled, she would begin searching for Beth.

She told herself the same thing later that evening by the side of the lake as she prepared to settle down again in her car. She would not always be this cold and hungry and lonely, she vowed, and choked back an unexpected lump in her throat. Jason was her friend now, and that was something to be glad about. And she would only have to spend another few nights in this miserable car before her apartment was finished.

She got as comfortable as possible in the darkened

interior, and soon drifted off to sleep. And as she sank deeper into oblivion, the figure of a man moved silently into her dreams, a man who held out his arms to her, offering safety and comfort and love. In her sleep Carrie stirred, reaching yearningly for him, and saw that his face was masked. He moved away from her into the endless shadows, but not before she had caught a glimpse of the soft dark hair falling across his forehead.

CHAPTER 4

EVERYTHING WOULD HAVE been fine, Carrie later
reflected, if the local police had not chosen that
particular night to cruise past her half-hidden station
wagon. And if the moonlight had not been quite so
bright, perhaps they would have overlooked the
telltale automobile hood sticking out from behind a
group of evergreens. But the police were vigilant, and
Carrie awoke with a start to find a flashlight shining
into her eyes.

"Miss?" an officer was tapping on the window.
"Wake up, please."

Carrie, blinked, sat up, and rolled down the window. If she stayed in Chicago's northwest suburbs
long enough, she observed wryly, she would probably
meet every policeman in the vicinity. She yawned,
and pushed the long tangled hair back from her face.

"Yes, Officer?"

"Don't you know it's against the law to sleep in
your car on private property? Unless, of course, you
live here?"

His statement was a question, and Carrie's heart sank. She had no idea that she was on someone's estate, especially someone who apparently owned an entire lake. Quickly she reached for her keys. "I'd be glad to move my car to a public place, Officer. I didn't realize I was trespassing."

"May I see your driver's license and car registration?"

Carrie gave them to him, her cheeks burning. Although he was treating her politely, it was obvious that he thought her a vagrant. And her disheveled appearance was doing nothing to dispell the image.

He studied her forms, and handed them back to her. "This address is from down-state," he pointed out. "Are you living in this area now, or just passing through on your way home?"

Home. The word held a hollow note of a promise just out of reach. She shook the sleep from her eyes, and explained the situation honestly. "I've rented a garage apartment on the grounds of Pine Tree Lane, but it won't be ready for a few days. That's why I've been sleeping in the car."

"Can you verify that?"

"Certainly." She fumbled through her purse for the rent receipt Matt had given her, and stifled a murmur of alarm when she could not find it. "It's not here, Officer. I must have lost it."

"Would you take out your cash and count it for me, please?" he asked, still polite, but Carrie could hear the growing suspicion in his voice. She did as he asked, tallying the miserably-small amount of pocket money.

The police officer flicked off his flashlight. "You'll have to come down to the station, Miss," he told her

45

decisively. "Unless we can get this straightened out there, we'll have to charge you with both vagrancy and trespassing. Follow me, please."

Why didn't they just handcuff her like a common criminal, and toss her in the trunk of the squad car, Carrie thought resentfully, as she followed the officer's car. But she knew that was an ill-tempered response. The policeman was only doing his job, and her situation did look a bit bizarre. *Oh, Lord. What a mess I'm in,* she admitted, adding a prayer for a clear head. Perhaps when they reached the station she would be more alert and able to explain her situation to their satisfaction.

When they walked in and met the captain, he looked at her even more quizzically than the patrol-man had. "Drugs?" he asked the officer.

"Don't think so," the first policeman began, but Carrie interrupted quickly.

"I don't take drugs, Captain. I can't take an *aspirin* without feeling drowsy."

"But you have no money to speak of, a downstate address and no local residence," the captain said. And, he could have added, a bedraggled appearance that did not correspond with her insistance that she lived in this affluent community. "I would suggest for your sake that we phone the landlord of this apart-ment you claim to be renting at Pine Tree Lane, and verify your statement."

"No!" Carrie interrupted again, remembering Matt's cold gray eyes. If he had been angry when they had collided on the road, how would he react now to be phoned by the police at two in the morning? She couldn't run the risk of rousing his rage or even worse, being tossed out of the apartment. "Please don't call him," she said with as much dignity as she could muster. "Couldn't I just stay here for the night?"

The two men exchanged glances, and the younger put a hand on her shoulder and escorted her to a back room. "Wait here for a few moments, Miss," he told her. "We'll see what we can do."

Carrie leaned back against the plastic couch cover, and closed her eyes wearily as the minutes passed. Would she never be free of problems? She rubbed her eyes, pushing back an exhaustion that almost sickened her. Perhaps the police would let her sleep here tonight, and tomorrow she could contact Jason and have him vouch for her. He would probably regard the whole episode as a joke and spend the next few months teasing her about being a juvenile delinquent. How she wished he were here right now. His quick-witted wisecracks would certainly cheer her up.

She must have dozed, for the next thing she knew, the young patrolman was bending over her. "Miss, would you come back to the desk?"

"Yes, certainly."

Sleepily she rose and followed him, stopping dead in her tracks as she rounded the corner. Matt Braden was standing in front of the captain's desk. She shuddered as she noticed the tense set to his jaw.

Matt's eyes flicked over her coldly. "Yes, she's my tenant," he said brusquely to the captain. "I'll take responsibility for her." He signed a sheet presented to him, and then turned to her. "Coming, Miss Craig?" he asked in a deceptively polite voice, but Carrie heard the undertone of anger, and stood uncertainly.

"I—I really don't think . . ." she began, but Matt strode to her side and took her arm in his iron grasp.

"Walk," he commanded in a fierce whisper, guiding her toward the front door.

Carrie was all too conscious of the patrolman's curious stare, but continued to match Matt's long strides. There was no point in making a scene and adding to her already troubled situation.

Once outside, Carrie spoke up. "I'm sorry they called you, but I'll be fine now. You can go on home."

"Yes, you're doing a great job on your own," he retorted, still grasping her arm firmly.

"Look," she said, fatigue and temper melding into an almost reckless feeling. "I asked you to let me move into the apartment. But no, you had to have it your way. So don't concern yourself about me now. Let go of me and I'll be on my way."

"Not if I have anything to say about it." Matt tightened his hold on her arm and pulled her around the side of the building. "Or would you rather spend the night in jail?"

"I would!" She twisted her arm away and turned to face him, a wave of anger filling her. "I'd rather live under the worst possible conditions than spend another five minutes with you."

He glanced at her bitterly. "You're even more stupid that I thought. What do you think can happen to a young girl when she's put into a cell with a derelict or two?"

They had reached her station wagon "Now come on," he said. I just signed a paper making me responsible for you."

"Well, I didn't ask you to."

Stepping back, Matt folded his arms across his chest, and Carrie could sense the rigid self-control he was exerting. Even in a hastily donned jean jacket and T-shirt he exuded strength and mastery of the situation. "Nevertheless, I was summoned and I'm here," he pointed out, "and it is almost three in the morning, and I have an early business meeting in just a few hours. So whether you like it or not, get into the car."

Carrie swallowed and reluctantly slid behind the steering wheel, and was surprised when he motioned for her to move over and got in the car with her.

"Can't you at least drive your own car home?" she asked.

"I took a cab. My car's in the repair shop, in case you'd forgotten."

"Oh. Yes." Carrie said, and as the engine groaned to life, she tried desperately to to collect her jumbled thoughts. It was a maddening situation. He was ordering her around, but at the same time he was offering her protection and some solution to her problem. What should she do? Accept his offer—whatever it was he planned to do with her—or fight for her independence and go her own way for the principle of the thing?

Deep down she knew she didn't have a great deal of choice. She was exhausted and wanted nothing more than to sleep and then soak for an hour or two in a hot tub. Perhaps he knew of a place she could stay for a few days. She gratefully admitted that was better than her own desperate solution, even though it meant she would be in debt to him. But she would repay him for any expenses. One thing was clear: she couldn't go on living in her car, no matter what she had believed earlier. For a moment she wondered why he even bothered with her. He certainly didn't have to. *Oh, how did I get myself into this mess*, she moaned for the hundredth time.

"Good grief, what a rattletrap," Matt muttered as they chugged into the highway. "I can't believe you drove the length of Illinois in a heap like this."

"I suppose it is a heap," Carrie pointed out, struggling to remain calm with her new resolve, "but I care very much for this car because it was given to me out of love—by my grandfather."

"Well, how can your beloved grandfather allow you to wander around the highway in a wreck like this? And sleep in it too?"

Her throat threatened to burst from the misery lodged against it but, as usual, there was no healing wash of tears to soothe the sorrow.

"My grandfather died two weeks ago," she said, quietly.

There was a small silence.

"And your parents?"

"Dead."

"I see," Matt said gently. "I'm sorry."

She looked at him in surprise. For the first time, he sounded almost human, as if he could understand, could somehow feel what it must be like to be alone and unloved.

But the moment passed quickly and she could see, even in the darkness, the hard line of his jaw. She took a deep, steadying breath. "Look, Matt, can't we be reasonable about this? Frankly, I'd like to know where we're going."

"I'll decide what to do about you tomorrow," he answered her. "For the rest of tonight, however, you'll stay at my house."

"At your house?" Carrie recoiled, shocked. "That's—that's out of the question," she said, hoping that her voice hadn't trembled. "I'm not spending the night at your house."

"Oh, but you are," he told her. "No tenant of mine is going to keep on living like a tramp. And just so you don't get the wrong idea," he added quickly, not letting her interrupt his discourse, "I have a live-in housekeeper. And I have a small brother too."

He spoke the last words with a surprising note of tenderness edging his words, capturing her curiosity. "A brother?"

He nodded. "Michael. I saw you talking with him."

"Michael is your brother? That beautiful little boy?"

He nodded again, a slight smile playing around the corner of his lips.

"I wouldn't have believed you were related," Carrie muttered inaudibly.

They did not speak again until he had pulled into his driveway and glided to a stop.

Carrie, almost overcome with fatigue, reached back for her brown suitcase, but Matt intercepted the motion and pulled it easily out from the back seat. He led the way into the house.

A heavy, lethargic numbness came over Carrie, leaving only a vague awareness of entering the house, walking up a flight of stairs, and entering a bedroom. Matt switched on a small lamp and looked at her.

"How long has it been since you've eaten?" he asked her gruffly.

"What?" She could hardly follow his words.

"When was the last time you had a meal?"

"I don't know," she shook her head blankly. "I can't remember."

He muttered something disgustedly and headed for the door. It clicked behind him, and Carrie thought she heard the sound of the dogs' paws in the hall. But

51

she was beyond full comprehension, beyond anything but a yearning for the mercy that sleep would bring. She would deal with her situation tomorrow. As soon as she sat on the bed she fell forward, her cheek touching the soft pattern of the coverlet, and she slept.

Matt returned only a few minutes later, carrying a hastily heated bowl of soup, but as he glanced at her small form, he saw he was too late. Only an explosion could wake her now.

He set the tray on the bedside table and stood over her for a long moment, his eyes tracing the heavy shadows under her long lashes, the delicate structure of her small features.

Carrie moved, and moaned softly. Matt reached for a blanket and gently tucked it around her. He stood for a moment more, gazing at her, a frown knitting his dark brow. Then, picking up the soup bowl, he went out of the room and quietly closed the door behind him.

CHAPTER 5

CARRIE STIRRED, AS THE FIRST weak sliver of dawn stole across her face, and opened her eyes. Sweeping her puzzled gaze around the unfamiliar blue bedroom, she knitted her brow in an effort to remember. What was this room, and what was she doing here? A clock nearby read 6:45. Was that a.m. or p.m.?

Struggling to a sitting position she suddenly caught sight of a pair of shiny, black dress shoes directly in front of her. Her eyes widening, Carrie followed the shoes upward. Her glance took in a gray, three-piece business suit, a crisp white shirt across a broad chest, a red-and-gray tie, and finally stopped on the man's dark features. Then, she remembered.

"Good morning," Matt said calmly. "I hope you slept well."

"No thanks to your forced hospitality," she retorted quickly. The bedroom door was ajar, and from somewhere in the downstairs distance she could hear the sound of pots and pans clattering.

53

"Good. I see you've recaptured your fighting spirit too," Matt went on, a tinge of amusement lighting his face, "but I haven't time to indulge myself in another match right now. You'll be happy to learn that I'm leaving on a business trip to California, but before I go, there are a few things you ought to know."

He set down a slim briefcase he had been carrying, but Carrie's attention was taken by his appearance, the firm lips, a barely disguised gleam in his eyes. He had a sort of *presence,* she realized—something that made her acutely aware of her own femininity. And yet she wanted to stay as far away from him as possible. She closed her eyes briefly, then realized he had been speaking to her.

". . . she's a nice woman," Matt was saying, "and I've asked her to see that you're comfortable."

"Who?"

"Mrs. Bennett, my housekeeper," he snapped, and ran a hand through his dark hair. "Pay attention, will you? I'm late already."

Carrie sighed. She was certainly having a difficult time concentrating on Matt's words. His well-tailored appearance exuded vitality, giving no indication that he had been up half the night, while she was aching in every possible bone, summoning her last ounce of strength to absorb the conversation.

"I paid your fine at the police station last night," Matt explained, "but I strongly suggest that you appear before the magistrate and plead your case this morning. I've left a letter for him explaining the facts but if you don't show up in court, it will be entered as a conviction, and you might come to regret having a police record."

"And you might come to regret having your

reputation sullied by a tramp like me, mightn't you?'' she shot back sweetly.

Matt refused to rise to the bait. ''You're probably right,'' he agreed smoothly, his long black lashes hiding the look in his eyes. ''I've only lived in this community a short while, and I would certainly like to guard my good name.''

''Well, you won't have to worry about me. I've decided that I have no intention of renting from a landlord who interferes in his tenants' lives.'' She hadn't actually decided any such thing, but now the words were said. She waited for his reaction.

''That's completely up to you,'' Matt went on, ''but I might remind you that you signed a six-month lease on my apartment, and if you leave, you will forfeit your deposit.''

Her mouth dropped. ''You wouldn't.''

''Oh, but I would.'' His tone was dry.

''But . . . but why?'' She could hardly believe her ears. ''Surely, considering our mutual hostility it would be awkward at best living on the same property.''

Matt shrugged, just a bit too casually, and she saw a disturbing glow in his gray eyes. ''Let's just say that a lease is a legal contract,'' he swept a mocking glance at her, ''and I, at least, have a deep respect for the law.''

He picked up his briefcase, turned toward the door, and then looked back to where Carrie sat, frowning and perplexed. ''By the way,'' he tossed in her direction, ''if you haven't anything more pressing to attend to today, you might want to clean yourself up. I'm rather particular about the type of people Michael meets.''

"You are disgusting!" Carrie said. The door closed and she heard the brisk click of his heels as he walked down the hallway. And then silence fell.

Soberly, she rose and wandered to the window. She was in a dilemma, and then some. If she left and looked for another apartment, she would have no money to pay her first month's rent. But if she stayed, she would feel at Matt's mercy, or his whims. Why on earth would he want to hold her to the terms of the lease?

A car door slammed and she glanced through the open window onto the driveway below. A white Lincoln Continental idled there, and as Carrie watched, a dark-haired well-tailored woman slid shapely legs out of the driver's seat, and stood to welcome Matt as he came out of the house.

"Hello, darling," Carrie heard the woman murmur, putting a possessive hand on Matt's sleeve, and turning up her cheek for his brief kiss. "You're late, you know. We'll barely make the plane."

"Just a small but annoying problem," Matt responded rather grimly, tossing his garment bag and brief case into the back seat. "However, I've handled it."

"In your usual efficient way, I'm sure," his companion answered, her voice almost purring.

Not responding, Matt seated her, slid in behind the wheel and shot the car out of the driveway. Carrie shuddered, hoping the Continental would not meet the same fate as his Mercedes, and then found her thoughts centering on the unknown woman he had embraced.

Although she had had only a brief glimpse, Carrie instinctively knew that she was a member of Matt's social set, the wealthy sophisticated type with inbred charm and grace.

In subconscious comparison she glanced down at her own rumpled appearance. No wonder Matt had voiced his wretched remarks about her appearance. Fortunately, she could revive herself with a hot shower and shampoo in the adjoining bathroom, then consider her problem from a more comfortable perspective.

One thing was sure. He had helped her decide what to do. There was no way she would stay on as Matt's tenant, she told herself as she relaxed blissfully under the hot shower. Matt's cocky reference to her as an "annoying problem" rankled deeply. He might think he had "handled" her, but he wasn't going to determine her fate any longer. She would try to leave as quickly as possible, perhaps today. She didn't ask herself where she would find the money for another rent deposit. She didn't want to think about it.

Finishing her shower and shampoo, Carrie wrapped herself in a thick terry towel, and studied herself closely in the mirror. Unlike most attractive girls, she was oblivious to her good looks. She had always longed to be tall, brunette and willowy, like the woman she had just glimpsed in the driveway, and was unimpressed with the petite porcelain-blond picture she made. She couldn't alter her size, but before she vacated Matt's house, she could at least cut her hair into a more manageable length. Hastily she took the sewing scissors from her suitcase.

Half an hour later, Carrie again studied her reflection and was immeasurably cheered. Her hair, freed of its heavy weight, had worked itself into a piquant cap of white-blond waves, clinging damply but neatly to her small head. "Very good," Carrie reassured her image.

But she dressed in a casual denim skirt and plaid blouse with growing nervousness. Did she dare descend to the kitchen and meet Matt's housekeeper? Just what had Matt told Mrs. Bennett about her?

Hesitantly she moved down a wide curving staircase into the foyer she remembered from her initial visit. Once again she viewed the partly finished home with undisguised admiration, then heard the muffled sound of a radio. Following the music, she came to the kitchen, a vision of modern equipment and shiny chrome, and saw the amply endowed, middle-aged woman busily peeling carrots at the sink.

"It's 7:50 in Chicago, and another beautiful day for you commuters," the radio voice said, and announced the Gospel music hour was coming up at eight. Carrie cleared her throat.

"Why—" Mrs. Bennett turned, then snapped the radio into silence. "Why, there you are, child. Goodness, I thought you'd sleep till noon."

"Am I disturbing you?" Carrie inquired quickly, but the housekeeper's broad smile dispelled her fears.

"Heavens no, just sit right at the table and I'll get started on your breakfast." She surveyed Carrie's wan face with a knowing look. "Let's see, perhaps some strong beef tea as a start and then scrambled eggs."

But as Carrie moved, the room began to whirl suddenly, and she leaned forward, gripping the table-top in alarm. "Mrs. Bennett?" she whispered, feeling the cold perspiration breaking out across her forehead. "I—I think I'm fainting."

"Nonsense, child," Mrs Bennett supported her

58

with a strong arm and eased her into the chair, but the concerned look in her eyes had deepened. "Just a little weak spell," she continued cheerily, "and if you put your head down and take several deep breaths, it'll surely pass in a moment or two."

Carrie followed the suggestion, oblivious to the woman who sped around the kitchen, preparing tea as if she were running a race. Within seconds, a cup of hot liquid appeared in front of Carrie, and the housekeeper lifted it to her trembling lips.

"Just a sip now," Mrs. Bennett soothed, "just a little, and we'll have your sea legs back in no time at all."

Carrie obeyed, and found that she was right. Miraculously she felt strength returning to her rubbery legs, and her clammy nausea disappeared. "I'm so sorry," she whispered. "It's embarrassing. I've never fainted in my life."

"Perfectly understandable," Mrs. Bennett commented wisely, "considering what you've been through."

Carrie looked up quickly. Had Matt told her everything?

"No, Matt didn't explain a great deal," the other woman read her mind, and a perplexed expression crossed her friendly face. "And I must admit that what he told me certainly doesn't correspond to what I'm seeing with my own eyes."

"Well . . ." Carrie hesitated, and then sighed. She might as well tell Mrs. Bennett about her arrival at Pine Tree Lane. It would be a decided relief to unburden herself to someone so kind. Carrie's words fairly raced over each other as she outlined the past several weeks, leaving out only the mutual animosity she and Matt felt toward one anther. The hostility between them was personal, and besides, she would never see Matt again.

Carrie eventually wound down, and realized that she had been eating a plateful of scrambled eggs during her narration. She looked at Mrs. Bennett sheepishly, and the housekeeper's eyes crinkled.

"Just a bit of psychology, getting you to talk so's you won't notice that you're eating," Mrs. Bennett pointed out. "Keeps the stomach settled. But I found your story quite interesting, Carrie. This sister of yours—if she's really been gone for fifteen years, why do you want to find her so badly? You'd barely remember her, I would think."

Carrie considered the words, chewing a piece of toast. "There are practical reasons, of course," she began. "I assumed after Gramps died that our house would belong to me. Oh, not to live in, it's run down now since Gramps couldn't care for it well these last several years, but I thought I could sell the property, and use the proceeds to continue my education. But after the funeral," her voice trembled slightly, "the lawyer told me that the property had always been in both our names, Beth's and mine, so I can't dispose of it until I locate her."

"And of course you'd like to finish your education," the housekeeper prompted. "What year are you in?"

"I've only attended college for about seven months," Carrie explained. "In fact, the professors let me take my finals early this year since I was leaving. When I enrolled, I took equivalency tests to see if I could pass some exams without taking the courses even though I had a state education grant. It's much cheaper that way."

"And did you?"

"Pass the equivalency tests?" Carrie asked. "Well, yes." She looked up, caught Mrs. Bennett's smile and returned it with a touch of pride. "I actually completed two years in one. And got straight A's too."

"I thought so," Mrs. Bennett nodded in satisfaction. "Knew you were a smart one the minute I laid eyes on you, despite what Matt . . ." She caught herself, and rallied. "Now you need Beth's signature in order to go on in school."

"Well," Carrie sighed, "I'm not sure I'm ready to return to college yet. I'd like to eventually, but right now, well, so much has happened and I think I need a little breathing space, some time to grow and sort things out." She dropped her eyes to her plate and noticed, bemused, that she had eaten another piece of toast. "I really want to find Beth for a totally different reason, Mrs. Bennett. She's all the family I have now, and I guess I need to know that she's happy, and that she has . . . forgiven me."

"Forgiven you? For what?"

Carrie shook her head. "That's just it. I don't know. But she left right after our folks died. Apparently, she didn't have much interest in hanging around for my sake. Maybe she didn't love me, or maybe it was something I did. Why else would she have stayed away this long, and never contacted me?"

"Rubbish!" Mrs. Bennett scoffed comfortably. "Child, you were only a baby then. What could you possibly have done to send your sister away? I'm sure, wherever she is, she still cares about you."

"I'll never know for sure," Carrie admitted and there was a ragged edge to her words, "not unless I find her."

"And you will." The housekeeper's words warmed Carrie's heart. "Let's see. How would one go about looking for a Beth Craig?"

"Beth Anderson," Carrie corrected. "That was her father's name, and she always kept it. Why, I'll ask around Woodfield, of course, but I'll also look in the telephone directories."

"In the telephone directories? For an Anderson?" Mrs. Bennett let out her breath, and went to a counter where several thick books rested. Carrying them back to the table, she set the stack in front of Carrie. "Look up the Andersons listed there," she directed, "and remember — that's only an area book."

Carrie leafed through it, shaking her head. "Two pages of Andersons in just one suburban area."

"Six in the Chicago book," Mrs. Bennett said, looking through a larger directory, "and five columns on each page and let's see, about two hundred names in each column." She looked up. "And did you ever consider that she might have gotten married?"

"This is impossible," Carrie murmured. "I had no idea there would be so many names to check. How foolish I've been."

"Just a little sheltered in that small town," Mrs. Bennett amended kindly. "Let's see. Matt's firm employs a few lawyers. Perhaps they could make some discreet inquiries."

"Oh, no," Carrie said quickly. "I don't want Matt to know about this." At the housekeeper's surprised glance, she lowered her eyes. "We—we haven't exactly hit it off well, and I wouldn't want to burden him with my problems." And she would die, she told herself, before she aroused his scorn again.

Mrs. Bennett chuckled fondly. "Matt's bark is a lot

worse than his bite, you know. He's spent his whole life taking care of other people, and I imagine he'd be happy to do what he could for you, too.''

Carrie resisted the cynical remark that rose swiftly to her lips. ''Taking care of others?''

''Matt's mother was only seventeen when he was born, and she abandoned her family when Matt was tiny,'' Mrs. Bennett explained, surprising Carrie with her openness about her boss's circumstances. ''Later, Matt's father became ill. Matt not only supported him, but kept him here till he died of a final stroke last year.''

''But where does Michael fit in?'' Carrie asked.

''A product of one of Matt's mother's trial reconciliations. I believe she stayed home just long enough to give birth to Michael, and then was on her way again.''

''How sad.'' Despite her dislike of Matt, Carrie felt a twinge of sympathy.

''It certainly was,'' the housekeeper agreed, warming to her story. Carrie assumed that she had few people to talk with, and settled back for a glimpse into Matt's past.

With the absence of a woman in the house, Matt's rearing fell to his father. There were plenty of conflicts between the two, the worst occurring when Matt reached college age and announced his intentions of attending an agricultural university out West.

''But Matt's father wouldn't hear of it,'' Mrs. Bennett said, ''and Matt eventually relented and accepted a football scholarship to an eastern school. He played left tackle on the varsity.''

Carrie thought that he certainly had the build for it.

''He'd planned to go out west to work on a ranch

63

after graduation, since a series of knee injuries had ended his football career," Mrs. Bennett continued, pouring them each another cup of tea. "By the time he received his diploma, however, Michael had been born, his mother was gone, and his father had already suffered his first stroke. There was nothing for Matt to do but stand by and go into business."

"That's rather a shame," Carrie pointed out, caught up in the narrative despite her attempted indifference. "If a person works hard at a career, surely it should be something he or she *enjoys*."

"Well," Mrs. Bennett shrugged, "he and Barbara have certainly made a success out of the imports business."

"Barbara?" Carrie asked. "Is she the striking-looking woman I saw from the window this morning?"

"The very same." Mrs. Bennett nodded. "She and Matt have been a team for a long time. They work well together."

So *that* was Michael's Aunt Barbara, Carrie mused, the woman who smiled only with her mouth, as he had said. Well, her smile this morning for Matt was certainly dazzling, she thought wryly. She could imagine the two of them lying together on the California beaches or hitting all the right night spots.

"And yet they haven't married?" she asked, and then bit her tongue. Why in heaven's name was she so interested in a man she, mercifully, would never lay eyes on again?

"Matt hasn't had time for marriage," Mrs. Bennett answered. "Too busy climbing the corporate ladder, I suppose."

"What about Michael?"

"That was when I came into the picture," Mrs. Bennett continued. "After Matt's father went into the nursing home, Matt moved the baby from their apartment to a place in Marina City. It's a twin structure in downtown Chicago, right on the river, so close that Matt could walk to work and be home in an instant if Michael needed him.

"I'd been widowed and didn't want to live with my married children. So Matt interviewed me just a few days after he moved in, and I'll never forget the way he looked down at Michael, sleeping in that basket. His eyes were shining with pride, as if his whole life revolved around that tiny little being, and he said to me, 'Mrs. Bennett, that child's going to have everything—everything I didn't have. I'll give it to him if it's the last thing I do.'"

She smiled fondly, her eyes damp. "So we raised Michael there, Matt and I, until last fall when he started second grade. Then Matt bought this property and we moved out of the city. The schools were better here, he said, and he wanted Michael to have the best."

Carrie wondered pointedly if *Michael* necessarily wanted to have the best and whether he was, in fact, actually getting it. His pinched somber expression at their first meeting made her doubtful.

"And so," Mrs. Bennett was finishing, "when I said that Matt's been taking care of people all his life, you can see what I mean. He provided well for his father and brother, continues to help out his mother whenever she turns up—although we haven't seen her lately—and look at this estate! Oh it needs work, but he'll accomplish that, just like he's handled everything else."

Carrie had no doubts. The portrait of Matt had been more completely sketched now, and it presented him as a capable but cold man, one who would possibly put his heart in a deep freeze in order to forge ahead. What sort of person would shut off the other side of his nature, the side that needed companionship and love? Only someone who learned long ago to live without these needs, she decided.

"Speaking of Michael," she asked suddenly, "where is he? Doesn't he go to school about now?"

"Michael's eaten long ago. He's usually up at dawn," Mrs. Bennett said, "but he'll leave just as soon as he finishes feeding the dogs. Matt did tell you about Mac and Tosh, didn't he?"

"Yes. Did he train them himself?"

"He did." Mrs. Bennett chuckled ruefully. "Dogs and horses. That's about as close to a farm as Matt will ever get now, looks like."

At that moment Michael came in the back door and stopped in his tracks. "Carrie . . . hi." A slow smile flickered tentatively across his features. "You look different."

"I cut my hair," she informed him. "Do you like it?"

He looked shyly at the floor and Carrie felt a pang of pity at his withdrawn small figure. She picked up his books and lunch box.

"Come on, Michael, shall I walk you down to the bus stop?"

He nodded, not looking at her and as they went past Mrs. Bennett she smiled at the two of them.

"Still waters run deep," she murmured, gesturing at Michael. "But I always trust his judgment about people."

Carrie felt a rush of gratitude. Obviously the housekeeper was telling her that despite Matt's apparent summary of her shortcomings, she had a different impression. Carrie hadn't realized how much she needed this reassurance, and it warmed her as much as the wholesome breakfast had done. She smiled at Mrs. Bennett in return.

Carrie was feeling decidedly better now, and she inhaled the tangy spring air deeply as she and Michael strolled down the driveway to the school bus stop. The dogs bounded ahead of them, chasing a stray squirrel, and Carrie wondered if they were Michael's only friends.

"Carrie?" Michael queried shyly just as the road came into view. "Remember those flowers, the ones you said we'd plant? Can we do it this weekend?"

"Why, I suppose so," Carrie answered thoughtfully. She hadn't yet decided when she was leaving, she suddenly realized, but surely she could stay until the weekend, and do as she had promised. At least Matt wouldn't be home, and it seemed to mean such a great deal to Michael.

"Good," the little boy sighed in relief, peeking up at her through his dark fringed bangs. "I like flowers. They aren't scary."

"Scary?" Carrie frowned, then realized that Michael had given her a rather subtle opening. There was obviously something he needed to discuss with someone, and hadn't felt secure enough to do so until now. "Some things *are* scary, aren't they, Michael?"

"They're not supposed to be," Michael shot back defensively. "Matt says only babies are afraid. He's not afraid of anything, you know."

Irritation gripped her. What sort of man would

make light of a child's fear, or try to shame him out of it? And yet she would have to tread carefully here. It would be unfair to take advantage of Michael's tentative trust in her by downgrading his brother. He needed the sense of loyalty he had already developed where Matt was concerned, but she could try to temper it by giving him a bit of self-confidence too.

"I'm afraid of driving, especially at night," she confided casually. "I think everyone's afraid of something. What's your biggest fear?"

Michael sighed, and his shoulder slumped. "Horses," he murmured in a very small voice.

"Horses?" Carrie was incredulous. "Why, Michael, there's no need to be afraid of horses. They're simply wonderful."

Then, catching sight of his dubious expression, she amended her statement.

"Horses are quite large, of course, and sometimes they look scary, but I'll tell you a secret, Michael." She lowered her voice to a conspirator's whisper. "You don't have to be big and strong to be brave, especially not with horses. You just have to know what to do."

Michael kicked at a stone. "I know what I'm s'posed to do," he said in a burst of impatience. "Matt's been giving me riding lessons all spring. But I'm too scared to do what he says."

And I suppose he threatens you with that look of ice too, since you just can't reach his expectations, she thought in sympathy. But instead she smiled. "What if I taught you?"

"You? But I quit my lessons."

"We'll keep it a secret," she assured Michael. "Just between you and me. We'll go over to the

68

stables on Saturday and see if we can arrange lessons. And then someday we'll surprise your brother."

"We will?" Michael looked up, and she could see his fear struggling with the need to win his brother's approval. His need apparently won, for as the school bus approached, he smiled tremulously. "See you Saturday, Carrie."

She leaned against the fence as the bus pulled away, a perplexed frown knotting her brow. *Now* what had she done? Committing herself to Michael meant that she would have to stay on, at least for a while. And how could she endure Matt's baiting or even worse his aloofness?

"See you Saturday, Michael," she murmured dismally, and turned toward the house.

CHAPTER 6

THE NEXT SEVERAL DAYS passed swiftly, and Carrie discovered that she was savoring every moment. With Matt's presence removed from the beautiful environment, she relaxed, taking solitary walks and reveling in the pastoral setting while keeping her observant eyes cocked for interesting stones, wood, or twig formations suitable for craft materials. Mac and Tosh, now her firm friends, usually bounded along, enjoying the outings as much as she.

Mrs. Bennett continued to cluck over her, cooking meals that awakened Carrie's appetite, and by the end of the week her pale face had taken on the glow of good health and sunshine.

"I feel absolutely wonderful, thanks to you," she told the housekeeper Friday morning as they watched two workers heading toward the garage. "But I'm dying of curiosity over what they're doing to the apartment."

"Haven't you seen it all week?" Mrs. Bennett asked.

"Not since the night I rented it," Carrie explained. "I didn't want to go back until I felt more settled about it." It had been a difficult decision, making up her mind to stay on, but now that the die had been cast, she found herself anticipating the move with excitement. "I wish Matt hadn't been so stubborn about letting me move in early," she remarked. 'I would have put up with inconvenient plumbing or wood chips all over the floor."

"To you, they're inconveniences. To Matt, they're code violations."

Carrie looked up in surprise. "Code violations? What do you mean?"

"This village is strict about housing standards," Mrs. Bennett explained, "especially now that so many landlords are renovating out-buildings and renting them. I believe God wants us to obey the law, and frankly, I'm proud that Matt is so careful. He hasn't been living here very long, and he's trying to build a stable home for Michael. You wouldn't want to get him into trouble with the authorities, would you?"

"No, I certainly wouldn't," Carrie murmured.

She had already involved Matt quite enough, beginning with his summons for reckless driving, and continuing through that horrible night at the police station. She had no desire to irritate him further.

At least the vagrancy and trespassing charges against her had been dropped. The magistrate had been understanding when she presented Matt's letter to him. He returned her fine, and ordered the matter stricken from the record. Matt need not worry that she had damaged his reputation. Sometimes it seemed to be the only thing he valued. That and his material

71

possessions. Knowing this, she had been careful to put the fifty-dollar fine back on his desk in the study where he would be sure to see it on his return.

Now she picked up her purse, and headed for the kitchen door. "Well, moving day can't come too soon for me, Mrs. Bennett!" she said. "Besides, I've caused you extra work, and I never intended—"

"Nonsense," the housekeeper scoffed. "I've enjoyed your company."

Carrie, still smiling as she drove onto the highway, realized with surprise that it had been a long time since she had felt this carefree. Almost every meeting with Matt had brought out the absolute worst in her. She was appalled at some of the things she had said to him and she still trembled at the thought of his imminent return. She would just have to put a lid on her temper once and for all. His behavior was up to him.

She could hardly wait for the weekend. She would be settled at last, and she would persuade Michael to visit the riding stables with her. Hopefully, she would be able to overcome his fears of horses. A glow of self-confidence replacing the woebegone look in his eyes would be well worth staying on for, Carrie decided, and she prayed that God would help her know how to reach him.

Now familiar with the route, Carrie cruised into Woodfield and went unerringly to Wood and Plants.

"Are you proud of me, Jason?" she asked. "I actually know my way through the mall."

"I didn't think it would take you long," he said, smiling at her. There were no customers in the store and he was on a ladder rearranging framed prints on the main wall. Carrie studied the arrangement.

"Try switching those three small ones around, Jason," she suggested. "The balance will be better, I think."

He did so, and jumped off the ladder to survey his efforts. "You're right," he told her. "The change makes all the difference." He slung a careless arm around her shoulders. "What would I do without you?"

"Oh, you'd find something," she teased, still feeling carefree. She had rebuffed all of Jason's advances, but the feel of his arm around her now made her catch her breath.

"How about coming with me to a singles bar tonight after work?" Jason gave her a pleading glance.

"Jason, I've already told you that I don't go to bars. What could be duller than an unwilling date like me?"

"I'll wear down your resistance, you'll see," he promised, and moved to the cash register. "By the way, we sold four of your items this week, two plaques and two driftwood pieces." He scooped sixteen dollars out of the register and handed it to her. "Thought you could use the money now instead of waiting till payday."

"I certainly could." A proud glow swept across her, and then as she turned to glance at the display table, her eyes narrowed in thought. "Funny, though. I could have sworn there were three driftwood pieces there. Are you sure of the count?"

"Positive. You brought two, and they're both gone. What's the matter. Don't you trust me?"

She looked up quickly, surprised to see that he was scowling. "Oh, Jason, of course I trust you," she reassured him. "Why, if it wasn't for you I would

73

never have had the opportunity to sell anything." She laid an appeasing hand on his sleeve. "Accept my apologies, okay?"

"Yeah . . . well . . ." He turned away. "Maybe we'd better go on a bookkeeping system or something."

Carrie punched her time card and went straight to work, biting her tongue. Jason had been so supportive, and she had practically accused him of cheating. And yet, as she waited on customers, her mind drifted back to the puzzle. What *had* happened to that third piece of wood? She remembered it clearly. She had created the pieces on the same day, and packed them all together. Had the harrowing events of the past few days muddled her mind to this extent?

She took a dinner break at six, said goodbye to Jason as he left for the day, and was relieved that he did not seem to be angry with her still. Making sure that the part-time worker had enough change in the register, Carrie strolled down the mall in the direction of The Brass Ring.

She found it without too much trouble, and was admiring a grouping of pewter figurines when a pleasant voice asked, "May I help you?"

Carrie turned to smile at the tall auburn-haired woman standing behind her. "You must be Liz Fields," she said. "I'm working over at Wood and Plants, and I decided to look at your merchandise. It's stunning. Oh, and Jason says hello."

The woman smiled back, a quick open grin that Carrie found instantly appealing. "Oh, he does, does he? And what else does the illustrious Jason King have to say?"

"Only that your shop is classier than his," Carries matched her lightness. "And I'll have to agree."

74

"Well," Liz pointed out comfortably, "my husband and I have been in business a good deal longer than Jason. Perhaps when he has our experience, he may gain a little class too!"

She grinned again and a tall lanky man came over to her side and put his arm around her fondly. "This is my husband, Larry," Liz said. "We were just leaving on a dinner break since our evening help has arrived. Would you like to join us, Miss . . . ?"

"My name is Carrie," she said, "and yes, I'd like to join you very much."

They strolled comfortably down the mall, and Carrie discovered that although Liz and Larry had been married four years, they had been in partnership longer than that.

"Woodfield was opened in two stages, you know," Larry explained, "And we got in at the beginning of the second stage, some eleven years ago. We spent so much time together at the store that I decided I'd better marry her; I desperately needed a buyer, anyway." Carrie joined their laughter, liking the easy affection between them.

"You must enjoy working here," she commented as they passed a display containing thousands of flowers that had been set up by the Dahlia Society, and watched shoppers examining the blooms. "There's so much going on all the time."

"Yes, we enjoy working here," Liz remarked as they turned into an attractively designed restaurant, and seated themselves in a booth. "If you can't find something to buy, you can have a wonderful time just sitting in the mall, and watching the world go by." She turned to Carrie. "I particularly enjoy the exhibits for children," she confided. "At Christmas

75

we have a Disney World castle built here, and each year Chicago's Lincoln Park Zoo sends its Zoomobile out. The children can hold and pet all the baby animals.''

"Oh, Michael would love that," Carrie said. "I'll have to bring him the next time the Zoomobile comes.''

"Michael?" Larry handed their menus back to the waitress.

"He's my landlord's little brother," Carrie explained. "I've just rented a garage apartment on the grounds of an estate called Pine Tree Lane."

"Pine Tree Lane?" Liz turned to Larry. "Isn't that the name of Matt's place?''

Carrie swallowed. "You—you know Matt Braden?''

"Yes," Liz smiled. "Isn't he a darling? We've been friends for many years, and we often order merchandise from his firm. In fact, Matt introduced us. When the store I was working for in Chicago sent me to a New York convention, I was terribly nervous, wandering around by myself, and in the midst of all the confusion, this tall, dark and incredibly handsome man came over and asked, 'Are you as confused by all of this as I am?' I loved him on sight, of course," Liz commented blithely. "He was the only one at the convention who cared whether I lived or died of terminal fright."

"Matt was a beginner too," Larry took up the story, "so he and Liz learned the ropes together."

"Boy, did we learn," Liz reminisced. "We stayed up till the wee hours going over catalogs, order forms, foreign trade exhibits, filling in each other's blank spots until we could function with some degree of professionalism. After we returned to Chicago we met again at a party. Larry was there. Matt knew him and introduced us.''

"And the rest, as they say, is history." Larry reached over and gave Liz a quick hug. "I had some money saved for a possible business venture; Liz had the know-how but no money.''

"So it turned out a beautiful merger," Liz finished for him.

"Now we're all waiting to see if Matt and Barbara merge," Larry commented.

"Do you think they will?" Carrie asked, and then stopped, horrified. What had possessed her to ask such a personal question?

Liz waved away her embarrassment. "I see Mrs. Bennett's been filling you in," she said, cutting up a juicy-looking pork chop. "Actually, Carrie, all of us are wondering about Matt and Barbara. He owes her a great deal, of course, but it seems pointless to marry just for the sake of a debt . . . ."

"Perhaps not to Barbara, however," Larry spoke thoughtfully. "Matt's made a lot of money in the past few years, and she's been urging him to form his own corporation. If he did, I'm sure he'd give her a large interest, but as his wife . . ."

"As his wife, she'd have it all, wouldn't she?" Liz agreed. "Yes, I hadn't thought of that."

"Well," Larry shrugged, "she'll have to push a bit harder. Matt hasn't made any moves toward starting his own company yet, at least as far as I've heard." He looked at Carrie. "Does he still travel frequently? I know he wouldn't think of missing the Paris trip every August, but with the new property needing work and Michael getting older, I shouldn't think . . ."

"I really don't know," Carrie shrugged with what she hoped was indifference. "I've only just met him, and—"

"And you don't particularly like him," Liz finished perceptively. "He can be hard to get to know. I've always felt Matt is much too high-principled for his own good."

"High-principled?"

"I suppose he is, especially when it comes to women," Larry mused. "They're always after him, especially at the trade shows, yet there's never been a breath of scandal associated with his name."

"He told me," Carrie couldn't resist being sarcastic, "that he values his reputation quite highly."

"I'm not surprised," Liz chuckled ruefully. "He learned his lessons well." Then with Larry's glance in her direction, she switched the subject. "Have you met Barbara yet?"

Carrie shook her head.

"You will," Larry smiled slowly. "She always protects her investments, and she's not going to approve of anyone as pretty as you living on Matt's property."

"Now, Larry, we're behaving like a pair of old gossips," Liz laughed. "Can't we find something else to talk about?"

They did, and after finishing their dinner in companionable conversation, the couple walked Carrie back to the Dahlia display.

"I've enjoyed this," she told them warmly. "I'm so glad I met you both."

"Come see us any time," Larry invited, and then as she turned to merge with the shoppers, she heard him call, "By the way, Carrie, what's your last name?"

"Craig," she shouted over the din. "Carrie Craig."

But Liz had turned away and Larry only waved. She realized her voice had been lost in the noise of the mall. But she would see them again, especially since they knew she was their friend's tenant. They certainly thought highly of Matt, she mused. Perhaps he reserved his cool behavior only for nobodies like her. She wondered briefly what "lessons" Matt had had to learn and why he felt so indebted to Barbara, then pushed the matter from her mind. After all, why should she care?

"Don't forget to set your alarm," Carrie told Michael on Friday night, peeking into his bedroom. "I want to get an early start for the stables tomorrow."

Michael almost quivered. "How about . . . next weekend?" he asked.

"Now, Michael," Carrie's voice softened. "I'll be busy soon, moving to the garage and then I'll have to work the next Saturday morning, so this is a good opportunity for us."

"Okay, Carrie," Michael murmured. Once again Carrie felt the urge to throttle Matt for his apparent heavy-handed treatment of Michael. *Father*, she prayed, *please help me help Michael overcome his fears*.

Carrie acknowledged gratefully that the little boy's mood had brightened by the next morning, and as they sped along the highway, he asked her several questions, his shyness seeming to drop from him. "Did you grow up on a farm, Carrie?"

"No, but I spent a lot of time on farms, Michael, one in particular. The owner raised horses for riding stables, and his two sons and I would often ride the yearlings before they were sold." The memory made her eyes glow. "Sometimes we'd have jumping contests. We would aim our horses at a fence and see who could leap over it first." She laughed. "I took a million spills trying to keep up with those boys."

"You fell?" Michael gasped, and Carrie winced. Why had she given him something else to worry about? "I never got hurt, honey," she reassured him. "I spent plenty of time learning first, just like you're going to do."

When they pulled into the stable's graveled courtyard, his lips were practically white. "There's Pete," he murmured at the sight of a grizzled old man. "He's sure gonna be surprised to see me again."

"Hi, Michael," the denim-clad Pete came up to the car. "Thought your brother decided the lessons were over."

"Michael, why don't you go and look at the horses for a moment." Carrie said, climbing out of the car. "I'd like a private word with Pete."

Michael wandered over to a corral, taking care not to get too close to the docile-looking mare on the other side, and Carrie turned to Pete.

"I'd like to give Michael riding lessons," she explained, "but we both want to keep it a secret from Mr. Braden, at least for now."

"Oh," Pete nodded knowingly, "so's Michael can surprise Matt at the horse show, right?"

"Horse show?"

"Big event at the county fair at the end of the summer," Pete explained. "Matt wanted Michael to compete, but the poor little guy is scared stiff. I told Matt not to push him so hard. Anyway, he told me a few weeks back that Michael was finished."

"Michael is not a quitter," Carrie said firmly. "Hopefully he will get over his fear, but whether he competes in the horse show will have to be his decision, don't you think?"

"Sure do." Pete looked over Carrie's small frame with a dubious eye. "You teach riding?"

"No," she admitted. "But I could demonstrate, just riding along with him. What would be the charge for two horses once a week?"

When Pete named the figure, her heart sank. Two horses were much too expensive. She frowned. Would her craft sales cover one for Michael? Perhaps she could just walk alongside him.

Pete noticed her thoughtful face. "Matt runs a tab here, you know," he pointed out. "I deliver him a bill every few months for his own riding time, and I could tally up your hours with the little guy there, and just tack them onto the bill."

"Oh, no." Carrie shook her head. "We're not charging this to Mr. Braden's account, Pete. I'll pay you myself each week."

He nodded. "Wouldn't be much of a surprise if Matt found out about it too soon, would it?"

She could trust Pete, she realized, and together they walked over to the mare. Already saddled, she seemed a good beginner for Michael.

"We'll just get to know the horse today," Carrie told Pete, "and maybe I can coax Michael into the saddle for a moment."

"Why don't you show me first?" Michael suggested hopefully, clutching at any delaying tactic. "You could ride Thunder, the one over there. He's the best horse in the whole stable."

"Thunder?" Carrie turned to gaze at the most

beautiful black stallion she had ever seen. Huge, with thick muscles rippling across his chest, he was full of spirit, dancing impatiently around the small corral. She would have her hands full controlling a horse so powerful. "Uh, he's rather large, Michael. Maybe I'll ride the mare instead, but only after you've had a chance."

"You said," Michael protested, "that a person didn't have to be big and strong to be brave."

"Well, yes I did," Carrie admitted, "but I meant—"

"Then show me," he demanded. "I'll ride Rosie here for you, but then you gotta ride Thunder for me."

You little rascal! Carrie thought. It was his trump card, and he had been saving it for last. He expected her to back out of the agreement now since Thunder was so large, and then he could forget all about the lessons. *Over my dead body* she thought resolutely—and it might come to that if she couldn't handle the stallion.

"You've got yourself a deal," she told the surprised little boy. "That is, if it's all right with Pete."

"Well," Pete cast a doubtful glance at her petite, jean-clad figure. "He hasn't had his gallop yet this morning, and he's sure rarin' to go. If you think you can handle him . . ."

"I can handle him," Carrie said with a confidence she was far from feeling. Pete shrugged and went to open Thunder's corral.

The next half hour flew by. Carrie had brought an apple and two lumps of sugar and, sitting on top of the fence, she showed Michael how to feed the gentle mare and get accustomed to her size and scent.

Gently she guided him all around the horse, making sure he petted her all over.

"Once you understand a horse, Michael," she explained, "you won't be frightened any more. You must always let a horse know that, although you respect his strength, you will never be dominated by it."

Just like with a headstrong landlord, she mused. How she hoped she had lots of carefree time left before he returned.

Just as the half hour was passing, Carrie managed to persuade Michael into Rosie's saddle, and she walked around the small ring with him, her hands reaching high to hold him securely. To her satisfaction she saw no signs of hysteria. Perhaps next week, or the week after, he might be willing to walk the horse alone—a small triumph, but enough for the time being.

Michael slid off the horse, side-stepping her attempt to hug him. "Now it's your turn, Carrie."

"What? Oh, you mean Thunder."

Pete was leading the stallion to the fence, using both hands to control the bridle, and Carrie shivered slightly in anticipation. Could she handle this powerful beast? Quickly she accepted Pete's leg-lift and swung into the saddle. Then, as he reared slightly, she grasped the reins with the instincts she suddenly remembered, and turned him toward the gate.

"I'll run him in the far pasture," she called to Pete, and narrowed her eyes against the sun. There were hurdles in that pasture, she noticed, and wondered briefly if Thunder had been trained for jumps. But never mind—a gallop would suffice, and he was certainly eager for one. Her fingers ached already as she held the powerful horse to a walk until they could leave the paddock and reach the open range.

As she released the reins slightly, Thunder surged ahead. She turned for a moment in time to see a white Lincoln Continental glide to a stop in the driveway. It couldn't be. But it was. She was just in time to catch a glimpse of Matt's shocked face as she shot past him into the pasture.

But Carrie couldn't spare a thought for his eventual reaction for she was already caught up in the exhilaration of the ride. Her head close to Thunder's neck, she gave herself up completely to the thrill of his long strides as the stallion gathered speed. It was as if she had never been away from this exciting sport, as if she were a child again, racing with her long fair hair blowing behind her, controlling a giant animal with the touch of her heel.

Thunder's mane whipped her across the cheeks and she leaned into the wind, savoring the feel of his powerful body. She was as one with this animal— free, boundless—and as they neared the paddock fence she headed him out again for one more thrilling round.

Once more Thunder responded to her unspoken commands, and as they circled the far end of the pasture she saw again the hurdles, set in place for a jump. Could Thunder take them? Oh, what she wouldn't give to experience once again the exhilaration of the leap, the breathless moment of weightlessness before the graceful arc was completed.

Throwing caution away, Carrie headed the horse for the first hurdle. Would Thunder obey the touch of the reins? He did! She soared magnificently over the first set of bars, and at the touch of her heels Thunder went for the second, clearing it with a foot to spare.

"Oh, you beautiful beast," Carrie murmured, feeling a rush of emotion as the big animal vaunted the third and last hurdle. "What a magnificent ride!"

Breathless, she galloped to the paddock fence, reined Thunder in amid a cloud of dust, and sat for a moment in the saddle, flushed with pleasure.

"That was some ride!" Grinning, Pete ambled over and took the lead rein as she finally slipped down. "I've never seen such control in all my born days."

"Carrie!" Michael's eyes were shining. "I didn't know you could ride like *that!* "

But suddenly Matt was behind Michael, and his clipped tones spoiled the moment. "Go and get into Barbara's car," he told Michael with barely-concealed anger. "I'll take you home, but first I want to speak to Carrie."

Michael obeyed, hanging his head as if whatever happened had been his fault. Irritated, Carrie noticed that his timid, pinched expression was back in place.

Matt strode around the gate and over to where she still stood. She noticed for the first time that Barbara was with him, leaning over the fence. Her thick, dark hair was caught back in a neat chignon, and a sardonic amusement twisted her lips.

But Matt was far from amused. "Just what do you think you were doing out there?" he hissed between clenched teeth.

"Riding a horse," Carrie told him matter-of-factly, willing the sudden powerful beat of her heart to subside. "And having the time of my life."

"Yes, and it could have been the *end* of your life," he snapped.

"Why?" she frowned. "He's spirited, of course, but I can ride and—"

"I mean that Thunder isn't a jumper. He's never been trained for hurdles."

"He hasn't?" Her mouth dropped. "But he jumped like a pro."

"Yes, and he could have balked and killed you. You were mighty lucky." His mouth was grim. "And what is Michael doing here?"

"We came to see the horses," she covered smoothly. "I'm sorry I upset you, Matt, but you needn't have worried about me."

"Don't flatter yourself." He was calmer now, but his gray eyes were just as cold as they had been at their first meeting. "I was worried about the *horse*. He's the stallion I'm going to buy, and you could have broken his leg with your foolish stunts. And furthermore, I don't want you frightening Michael. He's scared enough of horses as it is."

"Michael is afraid of horses—and most other things too—because of you," Carrie's resolve suddenly snapped. "You couldn't spare the effort to be quiet and kind with him, could you? Instead you forced him to like what *you* like, and now you're trying to shove your own failure onto him too."

Carrie saw his set jawline, the small pulse in his cheek, and swallowed against her rising fear. Then without a word Matt wheeled and headed for the barn.

Letting out her breath in a rush of relief, Carrie moved toward the paddock gate. Where had she found the nerve to stand up to him that way?

"Nice work," said Barbara, languidly leaning over the fence.

"What?" Carrie looked up.

"I said, 'nice work,'" Barbara repeated casually, but her green eyes were glittering with a sort of malice. "You're a clever girl, trying to get to Matt where it really counts."

"I don't understand what you mean." Carrie ran a hand through her tousled hair. She was disheveled again, as she always seemed to be whenever she saw Matt, and next to her, Barbara's tailored beige riding suit was the picture of elegance.

"You know he's fond of horses," Barbara went on conversationally, her voice grating on Carrie's nerves. "And so you try to impress him with your riding skill."

"I didn't even know he was home from his trip," Carrie said, "and I have absolutely no desire to impress him."

"That's fine," the voice went on, silky and irritating at the same time. "Because in case you do have any ideas along those lines, you might as well forget them."

Carrie saw the challenge in the older woman's eyes and felt an unreasonable urge to meet it. "Really?" she murmured. "And why should I do that?"

"Because you're in way over your head, little Miss Innocent with the big blue eyes." Barbara's venom was apparent although she kept her voice low. "I'm not saying Matt wouldn't enjoy toying with you a bit, but as far as any permanence goes—well, I'm all the woman Matt will ever need, or want."

"Well, how fortunate for you both," Carrie answered coolly, noticing Matt's shadow as he suddenly loomed behind her. "Frankly, Barbara, I wouldn't have Matt if he were served to me on a silver platter. I happen to prefer kind, loving men, not the sort who bullies anyone unfortunate enough to be smaller than he."

She turned, ready to savor her triumph, and saw to her distress that she had failed to rouse Matt to anger. Instead, his handsome face was creased in a mocking sort of mirth, and an inexplicable pain shot through her at the sight.

"Well put, Carrie," he smiled grimly, his hands astride his hips. "Now why don't you go home, and wash your face like a good little girl?"

Whirling, she marched to her station wagon. He had disdained her, ridiculed her, and although she shouldn't care, she felt the ache again, and recognized it with a shock of understanding. Despite his rude and arrogant treatment, she was attracted to Matt Braden.

CHAPTER 7

CARRIE SLIPPED THE LAST hanging planter onto its ceiling hook, slipped down from the chair and stepped back to take a look. Her critical eye told her that the effect was perfect. She gazed around at the rest of the room, and felt her heart warm again at the sight. Just as she had first suspected, the garage apartment was ideal for her.

Of course it was sparsely furnished, almost puritan in its lack of comforts, but perhaps, Carrie mused, the absence of clutter actually contributed to its charm. The gleaming wood floor, covered only by her yellow crocheted throw rug, was noticeable for its own beauty; the corner fireplace with the lone little rocker nestled close to it, presented a cozy picture. Since she couldn't afford drapes for the huge bay window, she had instead hung several planters at varying lengths on macramé cord, and the greenery seemed to merge with the outside landscape, bringing nature even closer to her.

Yes, it was lovely. All of it. But Carrie chewed her lip as she again faced her dismal financial situation. Even after six weeks, her earnings seemed to go more rapidly than she would have thought possible. She had cut her grocery allotment to the bare bone, but it didn't seem to help, and the car was facing a major overhaul. And she had to buy necessities for the apartment, most notably lumber for her bed base. In a magazine she had seen a picture of a platform bed that doubled as a couch, and had decided to build it. But the results were just short of ridiculous.

"Boy," Michael had honestly observed, "you're sure brave, Carrie. I wouldn't want to sleep on a bed that fell apart every night."

Carrie didn't either, and now regretted even the small sum spent on wood that wouldn't stay together, no matter how many times she nailed it shut.

Her eyes traveled absently around the room, momentarily observing the bright yellow telephone sitting on its orange-crate table. The telephone—now there was an expense she would have gladly done without, except for her need to find Beth. She had searched Woodfield to no avail, and now every evening she devoted at least an hour to phoning Andersons in nearby suburbs. But despite some interesting conversations, she had drawn a complete blank. If Beth Anderson had lived in this area, she had kept her identity a closely guarded secret.

Even more depressing than her slim budget, however, was the continuing hostility between herself and Matt. It hadn't ever flared into open anger since that day at the stables, but they had fallen into a terse pattern of keeping their distance, and greeting each other, if necessary, with a curt nod.

Yet living under those conditions was difficult too, since Carrie had to be on guard against unexpectedly running into him on the property or during her long soul-satisfying walks in the woods—not to mention the fact that as a Christian she felt increasingly guilty harboring angry feelings against anyone. Although Matt spent long hours at work, she was still never sure when he might be home. She discovered a bridle path and followed it curiously one day, but was dismayed when Matt and Barbara cantered into view. Barbara had smiled benignly as the two horses passed, but Matt had simply stared straight ahead, as if Carrie had no more significance than a twig, leaving her to stare wistfully at Thunder's massive retreating shape.

And yet Matt watched her. She was certain of it because she could often feel those ice-gray eyes boring into her as she planted border flowers or frolicked with the dogs. But he said nothing.

Sighing now, Carrie turned just as Michael clamored up the stairs and burst into her apartment. ''Hey, Carrie,'' he shouted, ''I got a great idea! Matt's gone riding and Mrs. Bennett is at the store. You can use my bathtub now if you want to.''

''Your bathtub?'' Carrie frowned, puzzled. ''Michael, why would I want to do that?''

''Well, don't girls like to get all perfumy and stuff when they have a date?'' he demanded.

''Well, yes they do,'' she smiled, ''but I'm just going out with Jason tonight. It's nothing special.''

''But all you got is a shower stall,'' Michael persisted. ''And I got bubbles and a plastic sailboat and everything.''

She resisted the urge to laugh. The idea of taking a

bath under Matt's roof was absolutely ludicrous. But she *was* preparing for an evening out, and the idea had a certain charm. Wouldn't it be heavenly to wallow in perfumed water, sink weightlessly into a warm bubbly foam, and ease her often-aching muscles?

"You're sure the coast is clear?" she asked Michael, her eyes thoughtful.

"I told you Matt's gone," he insisted. "C'mon, Carrie."

"I've got to be crazy," Carrie muttered, but on an impulse she grabbed her clean clothes and dashed down the stairs after Michael.

Strange, she mused as they moved down the path toward the house, that Michael had spotted the animosity between his brother and her, and knew instinctively that Matt would be angry if she invaded his home. She had never down-graded Matt to Michael; on the contrary, she had worked hard to build on Michael's innate worship of his brother, reassuring him over and over again that Matt loved him and was proud of him. Even so, Carrie had soon noticed that Matt's treatment of the little boy left a lot to be desired. He seemed to alternate between tolerant indifference and a firm-handed dominance, leaving Michael often confused and alienated, despite his need for affection.

She often felt that Michael preferred her company to Matt's, and it made Carrie uneasy. She knew she was good for him. He was becoming freer, more open with her, and he had begun to laugh easily in her presence. But she was not his guardian, and his basic loyalty should lie with Matt. However, there was nothing she could do about it, and now as they entered the house, she couldn't help enjoying the excited look in his eyes.

"I got it all figured out," he told her, lowering his voice to a confidential whisper, even though the only eavesdroppers were the everpresent Mac and Tosh. I'll hang around out in the hall, and if anyone comes by, I'll give a whistle." He demonstrated his newly acquired talent so shrilly that Carrie winced. "And then you can jump out of the tub, and hide under my bed."

"I thought you said no one was here," Carrie pointed out doubtfully. "Maybe I shouldn't . . ."

"Don't worry," Michael reassured her. "I'll take care of you."

She looked at him with affection. She was beginning to love Michael, and the knowledge brought an inexplicable wetness to her eyes. But she knew tears would not come; she had not been able to weep for many months, and she was in no danger of releasing her pent-up emotions now. Instead she broke into a run and Michael followed, smothering his giggles as they went down the long second-floor corridor.

"Oh, dear!" she muttered, stopping at the entrance to his bathroom. "I've forgotten my towels."

"You can use mine," Michael offered. "I've got one with a picture of Marina City on it—you know, the place where I used to live."

"Well . . ." Carrie hesitated, but the sight of the spotless tub, gleaming with invitation, made her forget her worry. Eagerly she reached into her tote bag for her bath oils and poured them into the tub with reckless abandon. As the steamy water hit the lotion, it exploded into fragrant bubbles, filling the room with a delicious floral scent, and Carrie sighed with pleasure. "Out with you now," she grinned at Michael and he grinned back before closing the door.

She was able to linger luxuriantly, though not entirely at ease, expecting to hear Michael's shrill whistle at any moment. Happily, their plot apparently undiscovered, Carrie dried off and dressed casually to return to her apartment. She opened the bathroom door. And then she heard him.

"Just what do you think you're doing here?"

"I had permission," she said, trying to sound calm when she felt anything but. "Michael let me take a bubble bath. I have a date tonight."

"With that character at the store?"

"How did you know?" she asked in surprise.

"A rather wild type, I've heard," Matt pointed out, ignoring her question. "Although I'm sure that wouldn't bother you."

With that, she turned and walked out the door.

Refreshed and perfumed, and determined not to be agitated over Matt's latest barbs, Carrie slipped into a pink and white dress. Looking in the mirror, she was happy with her reflection. Patiently, she now waited for Jason. There was a knock on the door and Carrie quickly answered it. To her surprise, Matt walked in, tool box in hand. She stood there dumbfounded as he moved past her without saying a word. He knelt on the floor, his teeth gripping several nails as he methodically repaired her bed base. Muscles bulged under his knitted shirt as he drove the long skewers into place, and eventually sat back on his heels with a small sound of satisfaction.

"Wh—what are you doing?"

"Repairing your bed base; Michael explained your predicament," he answered briskly without looking up. "Didn't anyone tell you that you have to use

94

braces at the corners if you want a platform like this to hold any weight?"

"No," she answered in a small voice. "What are braces?"

"Never mind." He stood and, lifting the heavy mattress as if it weighed a pound or two, deposited it back on top of the platform. "It should stay together now," he said and then turned to her.

She saw his eyes slide over her as he now took in her small pink-and-white form, her pale hair combed neatly into a cap of waves, and instinctively she turned to an arrangement she was working on, to look busy. But his next sentence stopped her motions.

"You look very nice tonight," he commented without a trace of derision. "In fact, you've been looking rather well for quite awhile."

His sincerity flustered her. "What, no sarcasm?" she shot back, then regretted her words.

But as usual, she had failed to penetrate his cool armor. "No, just an honest compliment," he answered quietly. "However, you don't seem to know what to do with them, do you?"

"I'm sorry," she apologized, "but you have to admit . . . well you haven't exactly been complimentary to me in the past."

"A situation I should remedy." He strode around the apartment. "This place, for instance. It's rather spartan but you've decorated it with real flair and taste. I especially like my grandmother's rocker there by the fireplace."

"Your grandmother's? But Mrs. Bennett said that it was just an old piece of furniture from the attic. I didn't dream it had any value."

"It doesn't," he waved aside her worry, "except a

sentimental sort of worth. She's been dead for a long time, but she'd approve of your using it, I'm sure." His eyes roamed to a grouping of Carrie's plaques and sketches, hanging next to a drawing Michael had done of Marina City. "You have an eye for interesting textures and patterns, too," he mused. "You ought to go on to school and develop your talent."

"I plan to, eventually," Carrie could barely conceal her surprise at his unexpected attitude. He could certainly turn on the charm when he chose to do so.

"And these pieces," he had moved to the long work center, and was fingering various items and studying them closely. "I've seen artesans by the hundreds in my profession, but these crafts . . . somehow they're different. It's the same kind of material, of course, but some curious element sets them apart."

"I like to think," Carrie spoke up somewhat shyly, "that perhaps they're special because they come from within me. They're a reflection of my soul, my heart, and that makes them unique. "

He set down a little floral plaque and turned to her, a small smile playing about the corners of his mouth. "And do you consider yourself so unique?"

"Why, of course," she answered, surprised at his question, and momentarily throwing aside her wariness. "God has made each of us special in our own way."

He leaned against the hearth. "That's not the way the world judges us, Carrie," he told her quietly. 'No person has value until he proves himself by accomplishments."

"Then the world is wrong," she pointed out simply. "It's not what someone can accomplish that gives him worth, it's what he *is*, deep inside. That's the only thing that matters. If you judge by the world's standards, then what value would you put on Michael, for instance? He hasn't *accomplished* much of anything yet, but he's still precious, one of God's beautiful children.''

She stopped suddenly, blushing to the roots of her pale hair. She hadn't expected to discuss her beliefs or Michael with him. He was staring at her, and she realized that to him she must have sounded like an empty-headed school girl. Well, he would just have to think so. He might as well know that they had a different set of values.

But he continued to pinion her with that merciless look. ''Tell me,'' he finally said, ''speaking of Michael, what do you think of him?''

The question had been asked almost off-handedly, but Carrie caught the alert interest hidden behind his words, and decided to be as honest as possible.

''He's very special to me,'' she told Matt, ''but sometimes I also feel sorry for him.''

''Sorry? In what way?'' Matt asked defensively. ''He has no parents, of course, although in Michael's case that could probably be considered a blessing. But he has everything else any boy could want.''

Except you, Carrie wanted to say, thinking of the toys and games packed into Michael's room, substitutes for the love he needed. She looked at Matt more closely, and saw the fine lines of stain around his firm handsome mouth. He did work hard for Michael's sake, she realized, and perhaps he was trying to do the right thing. And yet there was something vital that he had missed in the rearing of his small brother. Could she tell him in a way that wouldn't bruise his strong pride?

97

"I'm sure that Michael knows how very much you love him," she said cautiously, "but perhaps it would bring an extra dimension into his life if . . ."

"If what?" he demanded.

"If you also accepted him just as he is, with all his failures and fears, without making him *earn* your love." And what would Matt do now at this implied criticism? So much happiness for Michael depended on his reaction.

She half-expected him to flail her with a typically scathing remark, but instead he leveled that penetrating gaze upon her again. "You're a rather remarkable young woman, aren't you?" he said finally.

"Not particularly."

She looked down at the floor. His eyes were doing something strange to her pulse, sending it fluttering dangerously out of control through her body. She swallowed again the unfamiliar feeling. "Would you like some coffee, Matt?"

"I would." He moved away from the hearth and Carrie felt, rather than saw, the banked fires lighting his eyes. The air between them seemed charged with a peculiar sort of electricity, and she almost heard it crackle as she turned hurriedly toward the tiny kitchenette.

Matt followed her, and as she reached for the cups, she felt his hands placed firmly on her shoulders. "Carrie," his whisper was a caress, "turn around and look at me."

"Matt . . ." Her body was suddenly like rubber. "I—I don't think . . ."

Gently he stroked her upper arms with his fingertips, his touch sending shock waves of awareness surging through her veins. She could feel his breath, warm on the back of her neck, and her knees were as wobbly as a newborn colt's. "Turn around, Carrie," he murmured again, his voice languid yet insistent.

"No." Her answer was a sigh, belying the need that was rapidly rising within her. If she looked into Matt's eyes, if she found tenderness and longing there, mirroring her own sudden desire . . . Swiftly she reached for the cabinet door and swung it open. "I'd better make that coffee, Matt," she said, her voice holding little of the firmness she was attempting to muster.

"Just a minute," Matt's hands suddenly stiffened on her shoulders. "What . . .?"

He wheeled past her and flipped open the other cabinets, and Carrie caught her breath in dismay as he stared at her meager grocery supply. Silently he snapped open the refrigerator and examined its contents—a bag of apples and two quarts of milk. And then, with the familiar stony expression, he faced her.

"Just what is going on, Carrie?"

"What do you mean?" She returned his gaze and flinched at the suppressed fury written there. Where had his tenderness gone? Instead he gripped her with strong fingers.

"You know what I mean," he exploded. "What sort of poverty are you living through over here? Doesn't that boss of yours pay you enough to live on? Why haven't you said anything to Mrs. Bennett or me?"

"Matt, let me go." Not for anything would she reveal how heavily Michael's riding lessons and her search for Beth were draining her resources.

His hand caught her chin and moved it into the dusky sunlight. "Circles under your eyes. Are you going to wait until you faint again before asking for help?''

How had he know about that? ''Please, let me go,'' she protested again. ''Matt, you're hurting me.''

Swiftly he released her, but his iron gaze stayed riveted on her face. ''No one living in my home will ever go hungry, Carrie,'' he informed her curtly. ''From now on, you will have your meals up at the main house with us.''

''No, I won't,'' she defied him quietly. ''I don't live in your house, Matt, and I'm not a part of your life. I—I don't belong, and I'll never pretend that I do. And how I live is my business, not yours.''

They stared at each other for a moment, their eyes locked in combat. ''We'll see about that,'' Matt muttered, and strode out of the room.

Carrie leaned wearily against the wall, her mind whirling. What had happened? A moment ago she had been a piece of putty in Matt's hands, shaken at her own reaction to his touch, yet willing the unaccustomed warmth to last forever. And then, without warning, he had become arrogant again, bossing her around as if he owned her. Confused, she slipped out of the apartment. It would be safer to wait for Jason by the road, than take a chance on Matt's returning.

Her pounding heart had quieted somewhat by the time Jason arrived, and they greeted each other happily. ''Everything okay at the store, boss?'' she asked.

''Sold four more of your pieces. Only one left now.'' Jason grinned down at her, his eyes registering approval at her pretty clothes. ''That ought to make you happy.''

''It does.'' There would be enough money now for

Michael's next few riding lessons. And yet she was perplexed. It seemed again as though she had sold several more pieces than Jason was giving her credit for. She was almost certain she had brought eight items to the store last time, instead of the five he had just tallied. But she dared not ask him about it for fear of rousing his temper and spoiling the evening. She silently reminded herself again that she would have to start keeping records herself.

The two went to a quiet restaurant for dinner and ran into a few of Jason's friends, who went out of their way to pay attention to her.

"Where have you been hiding her?" one teased Jason, and he put a possessive arm around Carrie.

"Someplace where you'll never find her!" he shot back as everyone laughed. Jason made numerous trips to the restaurant bar, and Carrie became increasingly disgusted and uncomfortable.

And despite the good meal, Carrie's thoughts kept drifting back to Matt and the episode they had just shared. Once again he had shown her another side of his nature—the sentimental mention of his grandmother, and his tender concern for Michael. And had even asked her opinion, as if she somehow mattered to him. Finally, inexplicably, he had roused tender emotions in her, then fell into his old pattern of anger, destroying the moment. Why did he bother with her?

It was almost one a.m. by the time Carrie persuaded Jason to leave the restaurant. "Would you please let me drive?" she asked lightly, noticing with concern that he could barely walk to the door unaided.

"Don't worry, sweetheart," he read her thoughts. "I can drive under *any* conditions. You're perfectly

101

safe—from my driving, that is!" He gave her a crooked leer that said all too plainly what he was thinking.

Carrie clasped her hands tensely as Jason's car weaved along the highway. At least he wasn't a speeder like Matt. She wondered fleetingly if Matt were a heavy drinker too, but discounted the idea immediately. Matt would never allow himself to lose control.

Fortunately they reached the edge of Pine Tree Lane without incident, and Jason drove half-way down the path, then switched off the engine. The sound of the warm mid-June night filled the darkness—the chirping of crickets, an owl's hoot—and under different circumstances Carrie would have enjoyed the peace. But the car reeked of beer, and as she turned to Jason, she saw again the proprietary leer on his face.

"Aren't you going to drive the rest of the way?" she asked, trying to sound casual.

"Not just yet," he answered nonchalantly as his arm stole around her shoulder. "You're a beautiful little piece of goods, you know that?"

"I'm not a piece of goods," she protested, trying to sound firm. She jumped as his mouth met hers and he kissed her roughly.

"Jason, stop!" she pushed against his chest but his mouth pressed hers again. He held her tightly, making it difficult to move. With a final burst of effort, she freed herself and pushed open the car door.

Jason made a clumsy lunge for her, missed, and slid across the seat to follow her as she tore down the road. But just as he emerged, Mac and Tosh flew past Carrie. One shepherd instinctively guarded her while the other, teeth bared, prepared to lunge at Jason.

"Mac, stop!" Carrie cried, and the dog halted in his tracks, uncertain, at her command. But Jason wasted no time. Leaping back into the car, he shot it into reverse, and disappeared with a roar.

Breathing a shaky sigh of relief, Carrie buried her hot face in Mac's fur. Why did men take advantage of women, she asked herself, troubled. First Matt toying with her emotions, now Jason practically attacking her.

She bit her lip, trying to stem the familiar tide of loneliness. Would there ever be a man in her life who cared for her, cherished her for her own sake?

She rose and saw that Matt was standing a few feet in front of her. Wearing cut-offs, bare from the waist up, his face was hidden by the darkness. But his arms were folded in the familiar hostile gesture, and she sighed. Not another scene! She simply couldn't handle anymore tonight, not with her fatigue and misery almost out of bounds. She started to walk around him, but his words stopped her.

"Rather late, aren't you?" he commented caustically.

"You're not my keeper," she shot back.

"Well, you need one, with the company you keep."

Suddenly, at his words, Carrie felt a roaring in her ears, and from somewhere deep inside her a dam exploded. Tears of heartache flooded her eyes, and she lunged at him, beating her small fists against his bare chest.

"You—you rude beast!" she cried, gasping as the sobs became uncontrollable. "You judge from your almighty throne and never ask questions and always assume the w—worst!"

She could hardly breathe, and the ground had

started to sway around her, but she continued to berate him, gasping and weeping as her long-suppressed emotions took control.

Matt had stood silently, making no move to restrain her, but suddenly she felt his arms around her, and lips touching hers.

"No," she breathed, tasting her own salty tears. Imprisoned in his arms, she struggled but his closeness was having a devastating effect on her senses. Unbelievably she felt an answering strength within her, and her hands reached tentatively toward his face. A curious ringing sound whistled in her ears, and she felt as though she were drowning in the clean scent of him, the taste of his lips on hers. A sigh rose within her as she swayed toward him.

And then, suddenly, Matt thrust her from him. "Go on home," he muttered, shoving a hand through his hair. "Go on."

Bewildered, Carrie stared at him. It took a few moments to understand what he was saying to her. Then, a wave of rejection and fatigue covering her, she began crying once more, struggling frantically to gain control. "I hate you," she cried, wheeling and stumbling blindly to the garage. Once there, she slammed the door, tore up the stairs and threw herself on her bed. There the sobs came again, raw and ragged, as if something inside her had finally broken loose.

Just what was he trying to prove? She knew there had been no love in Matt's kisses just now. Just as there had been no real tenderness in his earlier caresses in her kitchenette. Both were only a means to some sort of end, something she didn't understand. And yet her own response frightened her. She had wanted him to go on holding her and kissing her. How could he bring about feelings that she had never experienced before?

Shakily she sat up, and for the first time noticed that the apartment looked different. There was a small antique table and lamp sitting next to the rocker, a beautiful arrangement. On her bed was a thick new pillow and comforter, and a little television set sat on the floor.

Opening the refrigerator she gasped in surprise. It was stocked with meat, fresh vegetables, and a small cake. And the cabinets too, filled with cans of coffee, staples, paper products. Someone had mounted a towel holder above the countertop, and a new electric frying pan stood on the stove.

Had it been Matt? Who else knew of her plight? Confused, she wandered to the open bay window, and as she looked down she caught sight of a shadowy outline disappearing down the path. The moon cast a pale glimmer on a pair of wide bare shoulders, and Carrie knew the figure was his.

Had he stood in the shadows of the garage, listening to the sound of her devastated weeping, leaving only when he was certain she was in control again? Carrie's tears began again, gentle tears that dropped softly down her cheeks. How could Matt be so kind—and so cruel—at the same time? And why, *why* did any of it matter to her?

With a feeling of resolution Carrie dropped to her knees beside the bed, her head cradled in her arms. "Oh, Lord," she prayed, "I've tried so hard to do everything myself, to make myself inside the way I thought I should be. But I can't do it. I can't change myself . . . and I can't change Matt. Please forgive me for not recognizing how much I need You. Please direct me, now. I'm so lonely and confused. And Lord, please change Matt's heart, too."

CHAPTER 8

EVEN WITH THE ASSURANCE that she meant every word of her prayer, it was a difficult night. Dreams of Gramps' funeral, Beth's abandonment, and Matt's anger caught her up in a confusion of contorted sounds and scenes. But by morning, Carrie felt calm and strong for the first time in many months.

She decided that she would return everything Matt had left in her apartment. Perhaps he had meant it kindly, but she couldn't accept it. No, she felt there must be a clean break between them. And so Carrie loaded as much as she could carry and slipped across the clearing to the back entrance of the house. Since it was early Sunday morning, she had almost an hour before Mrs. Bennett picked her up for the church services they attended and Matt and Michael would surely still be in bed. Carrie slipped quietly into the house and was busily replacing the canned goods in the cupboards when a shuffle behind her caught her attention. Turning, she found herself looking into Matt's eyes.

"What are you doing?" he questioned from the kitchen door. He was wearing a navy blue suit and tie, and a pale-blue shirt that set off the lightness of his eyes. A handsome stranger, Carrie thought, flushing as she recalled his kisses from last night. But she met his query with an armor of her own, born of the new-found strength flowing through her veins.

"I'm returning your gifts," she said, matter-of-factly. "It was a considerate gesture but—"

"It was not merely a gesture," he answered quietly. "I happened to be worried about you, Carrie."

"Well, there's really no reason to worry."

"Don't you ever accept help from others?" he asked, and she turned to face him, taken back by the genuine concern written across his firm features.

"Yes," she said with a slight smile, remembering her prayer of the night before. "I do."

"But not from me?"

"No, Matt. That's the way it has to be."

Matt's face closed into its familiar remoteness. "Well, then, I suppose you ought to know that I'm leaving this morning for the Orient and will be gone for at least ten days."

"Have a good trip." Carrie matched his cool tone. An awkward silence fell.

"Carrie . . ." Matt said finally, and made a move toward her.

"Ready to go, darling?" Barbara rounded the doorway, pulling on a pair of gloves and stopped short, surprise evident in her green eyes. She masked it instantly. "Why, it's the sweet child from the garage. Cory, isn't it, dear?"

"Carrie," she corrected, covering her own surprise at seeing Barbara so early in the morning. "Don't worry, Miss Breen, I was just leaving."

"Why, I wasn't worried in the slightest," Barbara purred.

In an intimate gesture she reached a hand to Matt's face and smoothed a lock of his dark hair back into place. "Shall we go, darling?" she murmured, ignoring Carrie's presence. Dismissed, Carrie closed the kitchen door behind her.

"He's despicable," she murmured to herself, and then tried hard to forget about it.

She wandered back to the garage and spent the next half-hour catching up on her chores until it was time to leave for church. Then she spent the rest of the day on a craft she was fashioning out of wood.

As she walked into the store the next morning Jason greeted her warmly. Carrie doubted that he even remembered their date too clearly and they settled into their usual comfortable bantering. But as she worked busily behind the counter, ringing up sales and helping shoppers with gift selections, her mind strayed again to the perplexing mystery of her craft items.

There was only one of her pieces left on the display table, as Jason had said, but the count just didn't seem right. Yet could she be positive? Yesterday as she had tidied the apartment, she had noticed that two more items from the work table had disappeared too. 'Have I been that careless?" she chided herself.

When the part-time helper arrived, Carrie took a break and strolled down the mall. Although she was meeting other Woodfield employees, Liz Fields was still her favorite. But she had seen Liz only twice since their first meeting and both times, she had forgotten to ask about Beth. It was dumb, Carrie told herself, because Liz had been at Woodfield long enough to have known many workers. And yet Carrie had sensed a hint of reserve in Liz, something not present at their first meeting. Perhaps Matt had blackened her character to the Fields. Or was she just imagining it?

As she reached the Grand Court, however, she was pleased to see Liz sitting on a bench. They spotted each other at the same time, and Liz flashed her charming smile and gestured to the seat beside her.

'Hi,'' Carrie dropped onto the bench. ''Busy, isn't it?''

''Fortunately for us, yes,'' Liz grinned, then looked at Carrie in concern. ''But you look a bit *too* tired. Is anything wrong?''

Everything's wrong, Carrie wanted to admit. But how did she tell a friend of Matt's that he was turning her life upside down? Instead she smiled brightly. ''Nothing's wrong, Liz, really.''

''Well . . .'' Liz's eyes were concerned, but she smiled and deftly changed the subject. ''Larry and I stopped by the stables recently to see Matt's new horse,'' she said, ''and Pete told us how well Michael's riding lessons are coming along. You ought to be very proud of yourself, Carrie.''

''You won't say anything to Matt about it, will you?'' Carrie asked quickly.

''Of course not. Pete told us it was a surprise. He also mentioned your own riding ability. I hope you're making use of Thunder whenever you're there.''

Carrie sighed wistfully. She had not ridden at all since the day she had taken Thunder over the hurdles; her cramped finances wouldn't allow it. And if even she could, other horses seemed to pale in comparison to Thunder's majesty. But he was Matt's horse now,

110

and she would probably never again have the privilege of riding him.

"I wouldn't want to bother Matt," she explained cautiously. "You know how he is."

'How he is? What do you mean?''

"Well . . ." Carrie's need to communicate struggled with her innate dislike of gossip. "Matt and I don't get along very well," she said finally. "We live in different worlds, have a different set of values."

"Even if that were true it shouldn't make you enemies," Liz pointed out.

"No, but of course there's Barbara too. I realize she's practically the Lady of the Manor, and she certainly resents my presence."

'Yes, she would," Liz murmured thoughtfully.

A small silence descended, and Carrie remembered about Beth. "Liz, there's something I've been meaning to ask you."

"Funny thing about Barbara," Liz went on, as if Carrie hadn't spoken. "She's visited our store twice in the past month. Usually she just sends an assistant over to take our orders. Why do you suppose she's nosing around Woodfield all of a sudden?"

"I wouldn't know," Carrie answered blankly.

"I wonder if she's got something up her sleeve," Liz mused. "Perhaps she's finally convinced Matt to go into business on his own."

Or to marry her, Carrie thought suddenly. But it was no concern of hers.

It was only later when she returned to Wood and Plants that she realized she had still forgotten to ask Liz about Beth.

Matt had been in the Orient a little over a week when Michael flew down the driveway one evening

111

waving a small box. "Carrie," he yelled, "Matt sent me a present from Japan! Special delivery! And there's one here for you too!"

"For me?" Carrie looked up in astonishment from the flower beds she had been weeding. Matt often brought Michael gifts from exotic places, for Carrie had seen the shelves full of souvenirs in his room. But why would Matt be sending her a present? Eagerly she reached for the box and unwrapped a tiny porcelein fan. "How lovely," she murmured. "Look, Michael, isn't it delicate? It makes me feel like a part of old Japan."

"There's a note too," Michael pointed out, obviously unimpressed with porcelein. And so there was.

"Carrie, I'll be home on the twenty-fifth," Matt had written in a careless black scrawl. "Please plan on going out to dinner with me that evening."

"Dinner with Matt?" she said, perplexed. 'Whatever for?"

"Maybe Matt's starting to like you," Michael observed shyly, then bounded back down the path.

Perhaps, Carrie sat back on her heels, touching the little fan with a reverent finger tip. Or was Matt simply feeling the effects of a latent guilty conscience? And what would Barbara think of the whole idea? Or perhaps she was accompanying them.

Whatever his reasons, Carrie decided she owed Matt her acceptance, at least this once. By returning the items he had given her, she knew she had upset him, and maybe it was her turn to put forth a friendly hand. Perhaps, keeping it casual, they could get through an evening without resorting to sarcasm, and Carrie remembered the commitment of her prayer. Only God could change her on the inside, she knew, and she trusted Him.

Despite her efforts to remain calm, however, Carrie found herself in a rising state of excitement on the twenty-fifth. She had few items of clothing to choose from, but had finally settled on a multi-colored skirt she had recently made, topped with a turquoise blouse that accented her blue eyes. She was almost ready to dress, wondering for the hundredth time to what elegant restaurant Matt would be taking her when the telephone rang. It was Mrs. Bennett, calling from the kitchen of the main house.

"I've just heard from Matt," Mrs. Bennett reported. "He's in California, unavoidably detained. He said to tell you he'd see you for dinner on the twenty-ninth instead."

"The twenty-ninth?" A surprising disappointment washed over her. "Did he say why?"

"No," Mrs. Bennett mused. "I assume he and Barbara had some last minute changes in plans."

Of course. Carrie thought. Barbara would have seen to it that Matt was detained from a date with her. In a fit of temper she hurled the colorful skirt across the room. Why was Matt, usually inflexible and domineering, simply putty in Barbara's hands? Liz had once pointed out that Matt owed Barbara a great deal; without her help he never would have achieved his meteoric corporate rise so soon. But did gratitude constitute an acquiescence to her every demand? Unless, of course, she was his fiancé, and he had always intended to include her in their dinner plans.

Well, she wouldn't go, Carrie decided. She wouldn't sit at a table with Matt and Barbara, watching them as if she were nothing more than a juvenile tag-along.

On the evening of the twenty-ninth, Carrie locked her apartment door and curled up in her bathrobe with a book. Matt could wait downstairs all evening if he chose, but she had no intention of meeting him. However, a few minutes after seven, she heard his quick tread on the stair, and realized with a shiver that he was coming after her.

"Open the door, Carrie," he commanded from the other side, rattling the handle impatiently.

"Go away," she called with a firmness she didn't feel. 'I'm not dressed, and I'm not going out with you."

"Don't be a fool," he muttered matter-of-factly. "Either open the door, or I'll kick it in."

With trembling fingers Carrie set down her book. Matt *would* kick the door in. Slowly she swung it open, lifting her eyes to meet his, and drew in her breath in surprise. Although impeccably tailored as always, Matt's face was haggard, lined with fatigue, and there were deep grim crevices at the corners of his mouth.

"You—you look so tired," she said impulsively, momentarily forgetting her irritation.

"I am," he said. "Now, get dressed. Please," he added wearily.

"I'll be ready in ten minutes."

"Make it five. I'll meet you at the car."

That's what I get for trying to take charge again, she half-thought, half-prayed, as she tore into her clothes. *I'm sorry, Lord.*

What a way to start an evening, she muttered. But at least Barbara was not to accompany them. As Carrie hurried down the path, Matt had already swung open the front door of the Mercedes. She had best keep her confusion to herself, she decided as she wordlessly entered the car.

They took off in the usual burst of speed, and Carrie gripped the seat with both hands. Matt saw her gesture, laughed softly, and slowed the car's pace.

"I keep forgetting you're not made for speed," he commented smiling, his earlier anger apparently spent. "That wreck of yours probably can't do more than ten miles an hour on a clear day."

"Did you have a good trip?" she asked, determined not to rise to the bait.

"A long trip," he amended, and she caught the note of weariness. "I'll tell you about it later."

"Thank you for the fan," she said quietly. "It's beautiful."

"It reminded me of you," he said. "Small and delicate. Although I noticed you were strong enough to return everything I put in your apartment."

She remained quiet, and they covered the rest of the distance in silence. Carrie had the uncomfortable feeling that Matt was only going through the motions, no more interested in being with her than he had ever been. Yet when they pulled up in front of one of the most famous French cafés in the area, she couldn't resist a murmur of delight. Matt smiled at her reaction as he helped her out of the car.

"I became hooked on French food several years ago on my first trip to Europe," he explained as they went through the café doors, and the maitre d' seated them with the proper touch of deference. "The company only sends me to France once a year now, at the end of the summer."

"But it's too long to wait between meals?" Carrie smiled impulsively as he accepted the menus.

"Right. Would you care for a cocktail? Or perhaps wine?"

"No, thank you." she told him. "Coffee will be fine."

"Coffee it is then," he decided. "That's just as well. I wouldn't want you falling asleep in the salad." Carrie laughed softly, amazed that they could be bantering so comfortably, and watched with admiration as he spoke to the waiter in flawless French.

Then she gazed around the beautiful room, intrigued by the enormous buckets of greenery, the crystal chandeliers subtly lit, the lounge chairs grouped intimately around a fireplace. There were sliding glass doors, too, leading to an outside terrace, and Carrie could see couples, the women in flowing pastel dresses, mingling under tiny lights that looked like delicate stars. "What a lovely place," she murmured.

She swung her shining eyes back to his, and saw that he was studying her intently, somehow pleased at her reaction. She thought again how very handsome he was. Several women in the dining room had already glanced their way, obviously admiring his rugged virility, and the ease with which he fit into these surroundings.

She wondered suddenly what *she* was doing here, in the company of such an attractive man, but pushed the feeling of wariness out of her mind. He was strangely charming tonight, and perhaps they could refrain from their usual bickering.

Fortunately, the conversation flowed pleasantly from one topic to another. Carrie found herself telling him all about her job, her friendship with Liz and Larry Fields, and finally her fruitless search for Beth.

He listened with evident interest, and Carrie was astonished when her first course arrived.

"Did you order for us?" she asked. "I never even noticed."

"I thought you might like the coq au vin rouge," he answered. "It's a favorite of mine."

"Let's see, that would be chicken," Carrie mused. "Ignorant fool that I am, I barely remember any of my French."

His intent gray eyes bore into hers, and she caught a hint of—could it be affection?—in his expression. "You're not at all ignorant, Carrie," he said gently. "Don't sell yourself short."

Her mouth dropped. Matt—her prime critic—offering her a compliment? She was at a loss, but deftly he turned from the subject.

"Did you ever consider that your sister Beth might not want to be found?"

Her fork stopped in mid-air. "What do you mean?"

"She left under rather unusual circumstances, I gather," he went on perceptively. "Perhaps she was running away from something. If you locate her, she may be forced to expose an episode in her past, something which by this time she's successfully buried. It could be a painful experience for her."

"I never thought of that," Carrie admitted, her heart sinking. "I've been looking at it only from my own point of view, wondering if she ever loved me, if I did something to make her leave . . . ." She looked up dejectedly. "I never considered her own wishes at all."

Matt covered her small hand with his, and she felt a little pulse throbbing nervously in her temple. She hadn't known he could be so gentle, so understanding, and a pleasant tingling ran through her. How nice it would be if she could keep him looking at her in just that way forever, his lips parted in a half-smile, his eyes playing across her as though she were the only woman in the room.

"It will all work out," Matt assured her. "Perhaps you will find Beth someday. Although your telephone bills must be outrageous."

She smiled. The magic of their intimate moment was broken. "It's worth it," she explained. "I'd sacrifice any material comfort to find my only sister."

"So I've noticed," he pointed out.

They finished their excellent meal in companionable conversation and as the waiter presented the check, Carrie sat back. "I can't thank you enough," she told Matt. "I've had a wonderful time and it was so unexpected, after the way . . ." She bit her lip, aggravated. Why had she brought up the past?

But Matt picked up her train of thought. "After the way I've treated you these past weeks?"

She nodded, embarrassed. His weary look, which had receded during dinner, had appeared again, and Carrie could have bitten out her tongue. He had been so relaxed, so *nice*, and now she had spoiled it. But instead he stood and pulled out her chair. "Shall we go out on the terrace?" he suggested. "Perhaps it's time for an explanation."

Surprised, Carrie accompanied him, noticing the feel of his hand on her elbow. They found a secluded spot overlooking the garden, and Carrie inhaled deeply and with pleasure, despite her sudden nervousness. "Time for an explanation?"

Then she turned to Matt and noticed he was lighting a cigarette. She had never seen him smoke, and knew

118

instinctively that he did so only during tense moments. She could see the firm set of his jaw in the semi-darkness, and felt a sudden urge to touch it, smoothing away the tension. But instead she stood quietly, waiting for him to begin.

"Although I'm extremely fond of Mrs. Bennett," Matt finally said, "she does have a habit of gossiping. I knew quite a bit about you, even before our conversation tonight, so I have to assume the reverse is true, that she's also filled you in on my background."

"Well, yes she has," Carrie admitted.

"Then you're probably aware that my father raised me after my mother ran off," he continued, and she heard the strained note in his voice as he stared into the darkness. "He was a strict hard man, and he believed firmly in the merits of frequent physical punishment—to keep me in line, I suppose."

"You were . . . a battered child?" She was heartsick at the thought.

"Well, I grew quickly," he went on ruefully, "and by the time I was in high school, that part of his control over me was finished. However, when I was still small, my mother had a habit of popping in on our home from time to time. And during these periods, my father was a different man. His harshness receded, and I could relax for a time, because of her presence.

"Inevitably, they would quarrel, she would leave, and then the, um, problems would begin again. Because of the situation I guess I loved her and hated her at the same time. Can you understand that?"

"Of course," Carrie murmured, a lump growing rapidly in her throat. The picture of him as a small vulnerable child tore at her insides. No wonder he was sometimes harsh and impulsive with Michael. What sort of role model had he had?

"The kids in the neighborhood used to taunt me about her too," Matt mused, "at least they did until I got bigger. That's one of the reasons I've tried to give Michael a more solid environment. However," he cleared his throat and Carrie could sense the effort he was making to expose his thoughts, "I felt a great deal of anger toward my mother. And she looked a lot like you."

"Like me!"

"Yes, tiny with long light hair, very young, of course, and she wandered aimlessly around the country, sleeping anywhere, or begging for a bottle of booze."

He turned suddenly to her, and she saw again the deep harsh lines in his face. "When I saw you that first day on the road, and the next few times too, it was almost as if I was seeing *her* again, and I took out a lot of feelings, feelings I never knew I had, on you. It was callous." He stopped again, and Carrie moved close to him, putting her hand impulsively on his arm. She could feel his muscles, tensed under the soft fabric of his coat, and longed to comfort him.

"Your mother . . . where is she now?"

"I buried her this week," he answered matter-of-factly. "When I reached California the authorities there had notified my company that she had been found dead. That's why I couldn't get home until today. There were things to be done."

"I'm sorry," she told him quietly, hating herself for assuming that he had simply lingered on with Barbara. Instead he had once more shouldered responsibility, as he always seemed to do.

"I didn't tell Mrs. Bennett why I was detained," Matt was explaining. "I was afraid she might mention it to Michael, and I wanted to tell him myself. He never knew his mother, of course." He stopped for a moment and then went on.

"Anyhow, she's dead now, and I think my feelings for her, one way or the other, were buried right along with her. The only thing remaining was to explain it all to you. I had intended to do that anyway, that's why I wrote you from Japan, but when she died . . ." He turned, and put his strong hands on her shoulders. "I've done you an injustice, Carrie. You never bore any resemblance to my mother, except in looks. And even if you had, I would have been wrong to be so rough on you."

"It's all right, really." She was grateful beyond words for his explanation. "I just don't understand why . . ."

"Why?" he asked quickly.

"Why you let me rent your apartment, and why you practically forced me home with you from the police station, if I triggered such unhappy memories?"

"Well," he sighed, running a hand through his hair, "that's another story, and one I'll keep for another time. Right now, Carrie, I'd just like to know that you understand."

"Oh, Matt, of course I do." Tears pricked her eyes. She raised her face to his and suddenly, unbelievably, he bent towards her and gathered her in his arms. Gently, with no trace of anger, he covered her face with his kisses, and finally, her lips.

She moved into his embrace, reaching behind his neck to stroke the soft dark hair. Matt's hold tightened at her response, causing her blood to race feverishly, then he stopped abruptly and raised his head. For a moment, he held her tightly, and she could hear the pounding of his heart mingling with her own. And then firmly, with a deep sigh, he held her away from him.

"Carrie," he muttered, "I'd better take you home."

"But . . ." She was bewildered at his rejection. "But Matt, what did I do?"

"It's what I almost did," his voice rasped in his throat. "I've just apologized for behaving like an animal, remember?"

"But this is different," she protested. "I don't understand."

"I know you don't," Matt's tone softened. "I'd forgotten for a moment that innocents still walk the earth." He turned abruptly. "Wait here. I'll bring the car."

In a haze Carrie slid into the Mercedes. A terrible fear wrapped icy fingers around her heart. She had read too much meaning into Matt's embrace, believed too readily that his feelings for her matched her growing love for him. For she did love him—she saw it clearly now—but the knowledge only served to increase her pain.

The Mercedes slid to a stop and Carrie realized that they had arrived in Matt's driveway. "Would you wait here a moment?" Matt asked casually as if nothing had happened. "I'd like to run in and check Michael, see if he's had any nightmares, and then I'll walk you home."

"All right." It was all she could manage.

She watched as he alighted and strode up to the front door. Then as he fumbled in his pockets for his house key, the door swung open, and Barbara stood silhouetted in the foyer light. Carrie heard them exchange a murmured comment and then as Matt went past her, Barbara came casually out to the car.

"Hello, Cory," she smiled, and Carrie caught the glint of malice in her eyes. "Did you have a nice supper?"

'Yes," Carrie murmured. "What—what are you doing here?"

"Doing here?" Barbara's tinkling laugh cut right to Carrie's heart. "Why, I stay here quite often, and soon it will be permanent. Didn't Matt explain it to you tonight? We're planning on marrying soon, thanks to you."

"To me?"

"Why, yes. The only obstacle right along has been Michael. He's so withdrawn, actually a rather dull child, don't you think? But you've been good for him, Cory, He's coming out of his shell, and will probably have no trouble accepting me as a mother-substitute. Matt's plan certainly worked."

"Matt's plan?" Carrie whispered, dreading Barbara's explanation, yet wanting to hear it.

"The moment he noticed your rapport with Michael, he had it all figured out. That's why he rented you the apartment at such a ridiculously-low figure. It should go for four times that, you know. Didn't you wonder why you were getting such a bargain?"

"And the things he sent over?" Carrie asked in a tight whisper. "The dinner tonight? The gift from Japan?"

"Gift?" Barbara's voice hardened for a moment, and then her tinkling laugh sounded again. "No sacrifice is too great for Matt where Michael is

123

concerned, as I'm sure you know. He's been anxious to placate the boy so he wouldn't cause trouble, and we could make our plans." She noticed Carrie's ashen face with apparent pleasure. "I'm sure Matt didn't intend his help as an actual bribe, Cory, he's quite generous, but—"

"Never mind." Carrie got out of the car, trying to keep her hands from trembling. "I don't need to hear anymore. I understand perfectly now." Swiftly she turned down the path, just as Matt emerged from the house.

"Carrie," he called, perplexed. "Where are you going?"

"The poor child has a frantic headache," Barbara said soothingly. "You probably plied her with wine, you dear man, but she's set on going home."

Carrie couldn't hear anymore, but she didn't care. Blindly, she swung open the garage doors and raced upstairs, hot, scalding tears flowing down her cheeks.

Now she understand exactly why Matt had forced her into his life. That was the "other story" he had said he would explain someday, the fact that she had been "purchased" despite his apparent dislike of her, because of her rapport with Michael. How could she face him again, knowing that all his kindness—and even his kisses—had been a sham, simply a means to an end for himself and Barbara?

124

CHAPTER 9

THE WARM SPARKLING HOURS of June turned into sultry July, and Carrie's mood matched the muggy, slow-motion tempo of the days. To move quickly, to think or plan past the next hour was an impossibility, and although she blamed it on the weather, she knew full well that she was suffering the inevitable symptoms of a broken heart. So much of Matt's previous attitude now made sense, fitted against the framework of the evening at the restaurant.

And yet she could not understand the knowledge that he planned to marry Barbara. Why had he treated her so tenderly if his heart belonged to another? Had he placed those sweet searching kisses on her mouth only out of sympathy or gratitude? Something deep inside Carrie wanted to deny it, to affirm without question that he loved her as she loved him. But she had to face facts.

The small vulnerable boy had grown into a cold sophisticated man, one who had seen many places and no doubt, had known many women. How stupid to think that someone as naïve as she could attract his interest, and be the catalyst for him to want to change, to turn his icy aloofness into lasting warmth.

And Matt was not a devious man. He would not encourage one woman's love while engaged to another. Barbara was an appropriate choice for him. Leery of closeness, he would certainly select a woman who placed no personal demands on him, someone as caught up in the desire for power and money as he was.

But reasoning didn't help her shattered heart. Like a sleepwalker she stumbled through the days, striving only to pass the hours so slumber would eventually bring a release from her suffering. She had seen Matt only once. He had come to her door the morning after Barbara's announcement to inquire about her health, and Carrie had answered his query politely.

"Sorry about that," she had said, keeping her head bent over her craft table to avoid drinking in his tall, rugged appearance. "It was just a simple headache, that's all."

"If you're sure you're all right . . ." Frowning at her, he had turned to leave and then looked back. 'I . . . ah . . . I'm sorry about things getting out of hand last night, Carrie. I realize you and Jason have become a steady pair, and I've no desire to intrude."

Jason? Where had Matt gotten that idea? Ready to contradict, she stopped suddenly. Perhaps it would be wise to let Matt assume that she and Jason were serious about each other. At least then she would have an excuse to avoid Matt. And she had to avoid him, she realized. It would only embarrass him if he sensed her true feelings, and she loved him too much to complicate his life any further.

But the days passed and no engagement announcement was made. Waiting in bleak numbness became so difficult that, one long hot afternoon, she greeted Michael's latest idea with a hint of interest.

"Why don't we go to Chicago?" he was asking plaintively. "You've never been there, and I could show you the Magnificent Mile where all the tall buildings are, and Marina City, and—"

"Michael, I could never drive in Chicago. It was horrible just going *around* it." She shuddered.

"We don't have to drive," Michael explained patiently. "Matt takes the train when he goes down. And I haven't been on a train in a long time. And I'm tired of swimming, and Freddy and Tim don't like to ride, and . . ." He sighed. "Summer's *long*, isn't it?"

Carrie had to agree. It had been the longest summer in memory, the days dragging out in an endless haze of depression. Maybe a trip to the city would temporarily suspend her brooding. "When would you like to go?" she asked.

Michael's eyes held a triumphant look. "Next Thursday," he decided, and Carrie nodded. She could probably switch days off with Jason. He was his usual affectionate self, although Carrie had rebuffed his further attempts to date her. Now she would have to relent, she realized sadly, in order to allow Matt's false impression to continue.

On Thursday they drove to the station and boarded an early afternoon train. Speeding through the suburbs in air-conditioned comfort, Carrie enjoyed the ride, and within an hour they had alighted at the Chicago-Northwestern station. It was a hubbub of noise, its corridors echoing with the sound of busy commuters, and Carrie clutched Michael before he could lose himself in the crowd.

It was then that she felt the familiar hand on her shoulder, and whirled to look into a pair of familiar gray eyes. "Matt! What are you doing here?"

He frowned. "I thought you invited me."

"Invited you?" Her heart was thudding dangerously at the sight of him. "But I didn't . . ." Suddenly the pieces fit together, and she looked at Michael at the same time Matt did.

"Michael," he said with a trace of annoyance, "Carrie didn't really want me to come along on your sight-seeing tour, did she?"

"Well," Michael stared at the floor as the crowds passed. "She would've, if I'd asked her!"

"Oh, Michael, you little devil!" Matt shook his head but he was smiling, and Carrie started to smile, feeling a growing excitement at the prospect of spending a whole afternoon with Matt.

"So that's why you wanted to come on Thursday," she chided Michael.

"Matt's always downtown on Thursdays," he explained brightly. "And, gosh, can't we *all* go?"

"It's okay with me, pal," Matt told him, a fond expression on his face. "I've already told my secretary I won't be back today. But what do you think, Carrie?"

He met her gaze with cool amusement, but Carrie caught another expression, too, and realized that, for some reason, Matt was looking forward to the idea as much as she. Her heart began to pound again. Just to be close to him, just for today. It was more than she had dared to hope.

"That would be fine, Matt," she answered softly.

"Consider it done." Matt propelled them out of the station and into a cab. "There are so many parts to downtown Chicago that a tourist could never see it all in a day or two," he explained as the cab bounced along. "But Michael has always had a fondness for the Magnificent Mile."

"When I was little," Michael chirped happily, "Matt used to walk it all the time, and he carried me in a back pack!"

"So I had planned on spending the afternoon over there," Matt finished. 'It's actually the section called North Michigan Avenue, starting from the Drake Hotel, and ending at the Chicago river. Visitors usually just walk it. There's so much to see."

"Sounds interesting," Carrie murmured. Frankly, she didn't really care where they went, as long as they went together.

But as they stepped from the cab just south of the Drake Hotel, she was suddenly glad that he had chosen Michigan Avenue. Cars and trucks whirled around her, the sounds punctuated by the shrill whistles of the traffic police, and there was an air of excitement among the swiftly moving crowd, hurrying down the sidewalks as if they all had somewhere interesting to go. Her enchanted eyes met Matt's, and she saw that he was watching her reaction.

"It's unbelievable," she blurted.

"This is just the beginning." He was holding Michael's hand and then, unexpectedly, he reached and took one of hers, covering it in his firm hard grasp. She felt her heart begin to hammer dangerously again, as they began their tour.

But there were too many things for Carrie to see; she couldn't remain self-conscious. They passed an interesting pale-stone building, dwarfed by the sky-scrapers ringing it.

129

"The Water Tower," Matt commented, "the only landmark left standing downtown after the Great Chicago Fire in 1871."

Down the street, elegantly designed, was the Water Tower Place, a self-contained high-rise in which one could live, work, swim, dine at famous restaurants, buy a Picasso painting or a greeting card, dance or see a stage play. Before they passed it, however, Matt stopped in front of a dark structure that rose to a dizzying height.

"This is the John Hancock Center," he announced, "the world's tallest office-residential building. Want to go up to the observation deck, Michael?"

The little boy beamed his approval, but Carrie stopped in her tracks. "All the way up there? I can't even see the top!"

Matt laughed again, pulling her along, and she subsided reluctantly. As the elevator soared upward and she felt the frightening flipflop in the pit of her stomach, she wished passionately that she had stayed on level ground.

But when the door opened, displaying the glassed-in deck on the ninety-fourth floor, Carrie moved toward the windows in utter fascination.

"I never dreamed anything could look like this," she murmured, taking in the aerial view of Chicago from every possible angle.

"Haven't you ever been in a plane?" Incredulous, Matt came to stand beside her, while Michael bounded to a telescope on the other side of the room. "This is just what it looks like from a jet."

"I haven't done much of anything," she said apologetically. "You must think I'm a terrible bore, Matt."

"On the contrary," he met her eyes. "I find your innocence very attractive."

"That seems like quite a change from the way you first felt about me."

"One is certainly allowed to make a mistake or two in life," he pointed out, "and I admit I've made my share with you."

"I've been content all along to be your . . . your friend." She bit her lip as the words rolled out. She wanted to be much more than his friend, but she couldn't change him and she wasn't going to try any more. Besides, he must never know how she felt about him.

"I see that now," he agreed quietly, then swiftly changed the subject. "It's a marvelous place, isn't it? Chicago, the city of superlatives. The world's tallest buildings, the busiest airport, the largest inland seaport and railroad center . . ."

"The whole state is a study in contrasts," Carrie added, covering her nervousness at his nearness. "Farther south we have coal mines, prairies, corn fields, and so much history, too, especially around Springfield where Abraham Lincoln lived, and yet up here it's so modern and bustling." She was babbling, and she caught his amused smile as he obligingly picked up the narrative.

"People call Illinois plain," Matt mused, thoughtfully, "But I've always believed that its very homeliness is what makes it so appealing. There's no pretense about Illinois. It's simply what it is, honest and generous and small-townish, and it's probably the only state in the union where you can see right down to the horizon." He gazed at the sunlit city beneath him. "If I can't have mountains to look at, then give me a beautiful blue arc of wide-open sky."

Carrie was touched by the feeling in his words. "I didn't know you were fond of mountains."

He sighed, smiling a little at a memory. "When I was in high school I ran away from home one summer and spent three months working on a ranch in Colorado. That's where I learned to ride. Even though my father eventually found me and dragged me back to the big city, I never forgot the majesty, the staggering grandeur of those mountains."

"Then," Carrie asked softly, "why don't you go back to them, Matt? Why don't you move to Colorado?"

He swung around to face her. "That's ridiculous, Carrie! A man like me has responsibilities, obligations to produce, expand. I can't just toss everything over for some dream."

"Why not?" she challenged him, reminded of the pressure Barbara was exerting on him to form his own company. "Matt, I wouldn't take away your well-earned pride in your accomplishments for anything in the world. But hasn't it ever occurred to you that you have an obligation to yourself too? If you aren't happy, then how can those who love you be happy?"

Her voice shook a little and she lowered her eyes, cheeks burning. Lecturing him again! Surely he had weighed every consideration before deciding how to live his life, and she had no right to interfere. But she felt his steel-gray eyes on her again.

"Wealth doesn't mean anything to you, does it, Carrie?"

"Sometimes I wonder what it would be like to live as you do," she answered him honestly. "But wealth—no, it wouldn't be what I needed for happiness."

"What do you need?" He had moved a step closer and if she put out her hand, she could touch his beloved face . . . . Instead she fought for control, swallowing back a rush of sudden yearning.

"I need to love someone, and have him love me back," she whispered.

He gave a short laugh. "You're a romantic, Carrie. You'll soon learn that it isn't wise to get too close to other people."

"I hope I never discover that." Her voice trembled. "I hope I never live like you—cold, aloof, using women for your own ends." Wretchedly she recalled how he had manipulated her into staying near Michael. But he misinterpreted her words.

"Are you accusing me of being promiscuous?" he demanded.

"I—I didn't mean—" she began, but he cut her off.

"Never mind. I once told you what sort of women I prefer, didn't I?" He shrugged. "Believe whatever you wish."

"I can only believe what I see," she told him softly, and felt her heart crack a little as he turned to face her once again, an odd mixture of curtness and vulnerability on his face.

"And what do you see?"

She took a deep breath. She could avoid the issue, she knew. She could tell him that she saw a strong, handsome, successful, probably brilliant man, and she would be telling the truth. She could tell him that he was so appealing that she had never loved anyone the way she loved him, and probably never would, and it would be the truth. But meeting his wary eyes, Carrie knew that Matt was somehow demanding her deepest honesty, and she turned to look out of the window.

'I see a courageous man,'' she said softly, pushing back an inexplicable rush of tears. "Someone who has generously taken on responsibility for others, but who's afraid to be generous with himself, to follow a star, to strip away the outside layers, and get down to where the real Matt is.''

She heard him start to interrupt but continued, knowing that he needed to hear it for his own happiness, although he probably despised her for her acute knowledge of him. "I don't know why this man is afraid to reach out, to touch another person's heart with his, but until he does, he'll never understand what life is really all about.'' She turned away, her eyes wet with tears, not wanting to see the scorn that must be written across his firm features.

"Matt!" Michael called from across the room, "come and look! There's a real cargo ship out there!"

Matt wheeled and strode over to Michael, and carefully Carrie pulled a tissue out of her purse. She had ruined this day for all of them, she realized. Matt would probably never speak to her again.

His attitude was stiff and withdrawn as the three of them went down in the elevator, but as they resumed their stroll along Michigan Avenue, he began to relax again, pointing out landmarks to Michael. Despite his anger at her, Carrie knew he cared enough about his brother to keep the remains of the day pleasant.

"That's the Chicago Tribune Tower, Michael, and the Wrigley Building,'' he was saying as they passed a jeweler's, and Carrie stopped dead, struck by something in the window.

"What are you looking at?" Matt came up behind her, brusque as usual, and she turned before he could see that her eyes had filled again.

134

"Nothing," she murmured, but he was adamant. "Tell me."

"It was just that little silver heart locket in the corner," she explained. "When my parents were married, my father gave my mother one just like it. He had both their names engraved on it, and she never took it off. Whenever I think of my mother now, it's hard to remember her face. But I can always remember that locket."

"What became of it?" Matt asked gently.

"Beth took it with her when she left," Carrie said, "at least I always assumed she did." She swallowed, then laughed shakily. "I seem to be terribly weepy today, for some reason."

Matt pressed a spotless white handkerchief into her hand and turned tactfully to Michael while she quickly wiped her eyes. Then as they began to walk again, he deftly changed the subject. Carrie was used to it by now. Whenever anything got too close to the armor Matt wore around his softer emotions, he immediately moved away. But she was not prepared for the new twist in his conversation.

"I wonder if you'd consider doing a favor for me?" he asked her casually. "As I told you, I'm quite impressed with your skills as an artist, and I'd like to see you exhibit your work where people could see it. You might be surprised at the favorable reaction you'd get."

"But . . ." Carrie realized that he didn't know she was already doing that at Jason's store, but he pressed on.

"There's a sort of county fair held every August in our area," he explained. "Craftsmen come from all around to exhibit and sell. There's a carnival, naturally, and entertainment and a horse show, but the exhibit tables are really the high point of the day. If I rented you one, would you be willing to display your things?''

"Well . . . '' she began doubtfully, ''I suppose so, but I'd rather rent the table myself.''

"I'll rent it,'' he told her firmly. ''We'll be partners. You just supply the wares.''

"Yes, sir,'' she replied demurely, relieved to see an answering flash of humor in his eyes.

They had reached the Michigan Avenue bridge, and as the traffic flowed about them, they went to the center and gazed at the river. Beyond Michigan Avenue were other bridges, a continuous pattern of arcs spanning the length of the river until it wound past their view.

"There's Marina City,'' Michael pointed to a pair of circular twin buildings on the river bank, tiny balconies on every floor adding to their interesting round shapes. ''They call it a city because you can do everything inside,'' he informed Carrie. 'You can even skate there.''

"Do you miss it, Michael?'' Matt asked suddenly, and Carrie watched them closely. She had never heard Matt question Michael so intimately, and wondered how the child would react. He had lost much wariness over the past few months, but . . .

Michael pondered the question for a moment, and then slowly shook his head. ''Carrie says you shouldn't love *things,* only people,'' he began.

"Oh, but Michael,'' she protested, but Matt silenced her.

"Go on, Michael,'' he said.

"So,'' the little boy continued thoughtfully, ''It

doesn't matter where I live, Matt, as long as . . ." He stopped for a moment and stared very hard at a small, red tugboat passing under the bridge. "As long as you're there," he finished shyly.

There was a small silence, and Carrie felt as though she had been handed a crown. Michael's words held a certain triumph, the beginning of a newer, closer relationship with Matt, and somehow she had helped it happen. Filled with love for Michael, she would have folded him into her arms, but Matt had gotten there first. Slowly he bent and kissed Michael's cheek, and the gesture, so painfully tender, caught Carrie like a knife through her heart. How she longed, would always long, for Matt to touch her like that.

Matt straightened finally, and looked at Michael. "Carrie's a very wise woman, isn't she?"

Michael nodded. "She's my friend."

"Well!" Matt looked around, "how about taking the sight-seeing boat onto the lake?"

"Oh let's!" Michael responded, and within minutes they were seated on the small commercial cruiser as it glided quietly down the river and into Lake Michigan.

Carrie watched the breathtaking city skyline view as the little cruiser bobbed along. She was grateful for the stillness, the peace of the open sea, the warmth of the late-afternoon sun as its rays sparkled and danced on the water's waves. She had needed this calming oasis of the spirit, the chance to pull herself together once again. Seeing Matt and Michael communicate, perhaps for the first time, in the language of the heart, had affected her deeply.

She eyed them now; Matt had taken off his jacket and tie, and rolled up his white shirtsleeves. His tanned forearms rested easily on the railing of the boat, and occasionally he would bend to point out something of interest to Michael. Michael stood close to his brother, hanging on every word, adoration written all over his small face. The breeze rippled Matt's hair, and as he threw back his head in easy laughter, Carrie felt again the sudden pang of rejection that had plagued her ever since she had met him.

She didn't belong here. Unwittingly, she had helped two troubled brothers into a deeper relationship, and she would do it again without counting the cost to herself. But now the way was clear for Matt and Barbara, and if she stayed on in her apartment, she would be nothing more than an unwanted relative in their new family structure. Oh, Matt and Michael would be kind to her, but could she live in Barbara's shadow, watching those mockingly triumphant eyes as they fastened themselves possessively upon Matt? Could she stand to be known as "dear Cory," a sort of fond mascot, when what she longed with all her heart to be was Matt's wife?

Throughout the rest of the cruise, through dinner at the top of another famous skyscraper, Carrie struggled quietly to keep her emotions in check. "It's been a wonderful day. Thank you, Matt," she told him as they finally turned into his driveway.

He peered at her over the top of Michael's head, a slight frown knitting his brow. "Is there something wrong, Carrie? You've been so silent."

"No, nothing," she said politely. "I'm just tired, I suppose."

"I'll be having a party the night before the county fair," Matt went on. "The house is finished now, and I suppose I ought to show it off. Liz and Larry Fields will be there. And Barbara, of course."

"Of course."

"I'd like you to come too, if you would," Matt told her. "I think you'd enjoy it."

"Oh." It would be the perfect opportunity to announce his engagement, she realized. Could she sit there in front of his friends, a wooden smile pasted on her face, as everyone congratulated the happy pair? Or would she make a spectacle out of herself, and embarrass Matt? "I don't think I'll come," she began, but he interrupted harshly.

"Carrie, for goodness sake, let me do *something* for you. I—we're both so grateful."

"I don't want your gratitude!" Appalled at her outburst, she reached for the door handle. "I'm glad both of you are happy, but . . ." The tears were pricking at the back of her throat. How could he be so blind? The last thing she wanted from him and Barbara was thanks for making their marriage plans come true.

"Well, look then," he ran a frustrated hand through his hair. "If you won't come by yourself, then why not bring that boyfriend of yours? The one you're so crazy about?"

"Jason?" The word fell between them like a stone. "I'll speak to him about it," Carrie said coolly. Drawing the remaining shreds of her pride about her like a protective cloak, she got out of the car and moved toward the garage.

CHAPTER 10

THE WORKMEN HAD DONE a proficient job, Carrie mused, as she watched the last of them disappear, making way for the caterers who were already unloading boxes from their trucks. She shouldn't be going to this party, she knew. She had resisted the idea, but in the end she had weakened. She had given the situation to God for His direction, and would try to do what she felt was right.

And she had to admit that she wanted to see Matt again. Like a helpless moth drawn to the flame that could destroy it, she was powerless to resist his magnetism. She felt that she must move on, get out of his life, but she would not think of it tonight.

She surveyed herself critically in the mirror, aware that blondes, under most circumstances, should never wear white. But the summer sun had done its work well for Carrie, burnishing her skin to a golden hue, streaking her hair to shining platinum, and the pristine ivory of the floor-length dress made her look like a

140

sophisticated ice maiden. Sewn by her own hand, held up by the tiniest of spaghetti straps, the gown bared her smooth tanned shoulders and hugged her small figure closely. Matt didn't love her, she admitted with a sigh, but maybe tonight he would see that she was more than just a child.

She had seen him only a few times since their downtown afternoon, and he had responded to her distant treatment with his usual self-possessed coolness. Only this morning, when he had come to collect the boxes she had packed for tomorrow's fair exhibit, had he shown any signs of impatience.

"What's the matter with you lately, Carrie?" he had said. "If I've done something to anger you, I'd rather you spill it instead of acting like this."

She hadn't been able to answer, and he had loaded his car and sped off.

Now, careful not to soil her hem, she went down the path to the main house. Jason would be meeting her later at the party, and Carrie was glad of a respite; she feared what effect her gown would have on Jason. Her eyes warmed in admiration as she approached the yard. Once overgrown and weedy, the summer land-scaping crew had created a miracle, taming the grounds to perfection. Chinese lanterns and tiny sparklers hung from wires criss-crossing the wide clipped lawn. Along one side of the yard, beside the pool, a six-piece band was playing beautiful waltzes and lively fox trots. She had never attended such a lavish party, and she was glad for the experience, despite the inevitable agony she would have to suffer whenever Matt appeared.

The sound of laughter at the patio door caught her attention. Several couples were coming out onto the

141

lawn, and her heart began to pound uneasily as she caught sight of Matt. The white dinner jacket set off his tanned ruggedness. She turned, suddenly wanting to escape before she was seen.

"Carrie, hello. Good to see you!" Larry Fields called from the doorway. It was too late now, and as she saw Matt glance at her, then sweep his gray gaze across her in stunned amazement, courage flooded her once more. She had not left him unmoved; at least she would have that consolation. Squaring her shoulders, she walked confidently over to the group.

Matt had recovered. "This is Miss Craig, my tenant." He introduced her as if she were a distant acquaintance. She felt a surge of disappointment at his manner, but murmured graciously to each guest. Most of them were business associates, obviously impressed with Matt's home.

"I would have bought this place too, if she came with it!" one portly gentleman told Matt, winking at Carrie.

Another chuckled. "You've done your usual superb job with it, too, Matt. And what's next on the horizon? Any truth to the rumor that you're starting your own company?"

"Well," Matt began, as Barbara drifted toward them.

"Hello, Cory dear, how precious you look." She was a vision of cosmopolitan elegance in a shimmering, black, designer dress, and Carrie suddenly felt childish beside her, like a little girl caught masquerading in her mother's clothes. Barbara laid her hand on Matt's sleeve.

"The Bergens are here, darling, and the Hardings too," she murmured, all too conscious of her role as hostess. "I thought you would want to greet them personally."

"Of course," Matt nodded. "Excuse me." And as he moved away, Carrie felt another jab of regret. *Well, what did you expect?* she asked herself angrily. Was Matt supposed to fall down in adoration just because she looked a little older than usual?

"You look absolutely ravishing." Liz put a friendly arm around her. "Where on earth do you buy such beautiful clothes?"

"I make most of them, including this," Carrie admitted.

Larry whistled in appreciation. "Good heavens. We have another Edith Head on our hands!"

Buoyed by their kindness, Carrie accompanied them to a corner table.

"Hi, Carrie!" Michael appeared, dressed in a dark blue suit, and flashed an excited smile.

"Michael—you look cleaner than you have all summer!" she teased, giving herself up to the laughter and camraderie, refusing to glance again at the patio door. She *would* have good time tonight!

Jason arrived a short time later, and as Matt escorted him to their table, Carrie felt a wave of perverse pleasure. Jason was looking his most attractive, and she was glad she had invited him, no matter what Matt would think.

"Hi, sweetheart!" he planted a warm kiss on her lips. "You're gorgeous. Has anyone mentioned it?"

"Everyone has," Liz laughed. "Get in line, Jason."

"That I will. The prize is worth it." He draped an arm casually around Carrie's shoulders, running his thumb back and forth along her arm, and she saw out

143

of the corner of her eye that Matt had moved a few feet away. Apparently engrossed in conversation, his eyes occasionally flicked her way, and she was obstinately satisfied. He had noticed, after all!

Giving Carrie an approving wink, Mrs. Bennett moved past their table with a tray of hors d'eurves.

"Jason," Carrie murmured into his ear, "be a good sport and ask that lady to dance. She's Matt's housekeeper, and she'd give her right arm to waltz with someone like you."

"Are you kidding?" Jason was incredulous, but at her pleading glance, he arose good-naturedly.

Carrie watched them for a moment, and then she felt a warm hand on her shoulder. When she did not look up, Matt sat down beside her.

Slowly she raised her eyes and saw that he was staring at her with the intent gray gaze she had learned to love.

"Carrie," he said, somewhat unsteadily. "I've never seen you looking so beautiful."

"Thank you," she whispered, aware that her voice was trembling. "I—I'm glad you noticed."

"I notice everything about you, Carrie," he said quietly. "I always have, ever since that first day on the road."

For what purpose would he rake up old memories? She would have a lifetime to remember, but she would be alone, and she had to put a stop to his words before they overwhelmed her.

"The past is dead and buried," she told him. "It has no bearing on us now."

"Doesn't it?" he asked. "Or are you simply avoiding reality?"

"Avoiding reality?" It was impossible to look at

144

him. "No, I'm facing it, Matt. I know I have no place in your life, nor you in mine."

"We'll see about that," he muttered. With one hand he turned her chin firmly upward, forcing her to face him.

"Look at me, Carrie," he commanded quietly. Slowly she met his clear gaze, and felt her heart pounding. If he kissed her, she couldn't bear it.

"Please don't play with me, Matt," she murmured miserably.

"It's you who are playing, Carrie," There was a trace of something—was it sympathy?—in his voice. "Tonight, after this party, I'll meet you at the garage."

"You'll do what?" she said, astonished.

"There are things I have to tell you," Matt began, but just then Barbara came gliding up to them.

"Really, Matt!" her brittle voice was irritated, "the waiters are ready to serve. We *do* have guests!"

"Yes, I'm aware of that," he stated, letting go of Carrie. Then, as Barbara stalked ahead, he turned back. "Tonight, Carrie, after the party." He brushed her cheeks with his fingertips and moved away, leaving Carrie staring after him.

There are things I have to tell you, Matt had said, and there had been a sympathetic note in his voice. Of course, she reasoned wildly. After his engagement announcement, Matt would be decent enough to inform her of his future plans, perhaps terminate her lease. She put her palms against her hot cheeks. How could she get through the rest of this evening?

Jason appeared at her side. "You okay, sweetheart?" he slung his arm around her.

"Just a little warm," she swallowed convulsively. "Jason, would you mind if I went home?"

"What, and miss the meal of the century?" He grinned. "I sneaked a look at the place cards, kid. We're dining at the table of His Highness!"

It couldn't be true, but it was. As they entered the house, Carrie saw in distress that tables had been set throughout the downstairs room for four or five couples each, and that she, Jason and the Fields were to share Matt's table. She felt a heightened urge to flee, but controlled herself with an effort, as Matt and Barbara appeared, arm in arm.

The dinner looked exquisite, starting with chilled melon and strawberries, proceeding through onion soup to a beautiful salad, and finally a choice of roast duck or prime rib. To Carrie, it was all tasteless. *Tonight*. Matt's words kept echoing in her mind.

"What, nothing French?" Liz teased Matt with affection, and he smiled easily.

"Not everyone shares my tastes," he admitted.

Carrie could not bear to look at him, but she noticed that he seemed to be enjoying himself immensely. The guests' visible approval had apparently thawed his usual reserve, and his smile made him even more attractive. The other women at the party seemed to think so too. She had noticed their attention lavished upon him all evening, and could understand why Barbara was preening herself like a satisfied peacock. Why shouldn't she, considering that she had finally captured her prey? Her magnanimity even extended to Carrie, for she leaned over the table during the entree, and complimented her on her white dress.

"She made it herself," Liz pointed out with relish. "Carrie is a girl of many talents. You must enjoy having her work for you, Jason."

"I do." Jason covered Carrie's hand with his. "She

146

certainly livens up the place." Carrie flushed, aware of Matt's cool stare.

"And by the way," Liz went on cheerfully, "I have to commend you on that exquisite selection of loss leaders at the entrance of your shop, Jason. I don't know where you get them, but I'd give a lot to have the same pieces. Frankly, I don't see how you can afford to sell them at such a low price— "

"Please, no business talk tonight," Jason waved away her remarks, but Carrie had seen him stiffen, and she looked at Liz, bewildered.

"Loss leaders? What are those?"

"Oh," Liz salted her prime rib, "those are items, Carrie, that a merchant sells at a price far below their true worth. It's a sales trick. Put a real bargain at the door of your store, or advertise one the way the supermarkets do, and it lures customers. Once inside, they will probably buy something else as well."

Carrie frowned. Liz was talking about her crafts. Was she saying that Jason had tricked her, purchased her material at far under its value to attract customers? She looked at Jason, and saw that his face had gone pale. Matt entered the conversation.

"What do these loss leaders look like, Liz?" he asked, alert as a hunter stalking his quarry.

"Soft, touching little crafts," Larry answered. "We've both marveled at them. Basically, they're pieces of nature, twigs, bleached bark, driftwood and the like, but whoever designs them has an enchanting way of making them come alive."

"I see." Swiftly Matt rose, went to the buffet and removed two small items from a drawer. Carrie's mouth dropped. So that was where those two pieces had gone, the day she had missed them from her table.

Matt had taken them. But why? "These are the items you're talking about, aren't they?" he asked, his voice grim as he handed them to Liz.

"Why, yes, aren't they charming?" Liz asked and then narrowed her eyes. "But you knew about this already, didn't you, Matt?"

But Matt's eyes were fixed on Jason, and as Carrie's heart sank, Jason edged uncomfortably away from her.

"Jason?" she asked in a whisper, "Jason, have you been cheating me?"

He shrugged. "Not really. I was intending to make it up to you eventually."

"And the count?" she prodded, not wanting to believe what must surely be true. "Am I making a mistake? Or were you?"

His silence confirmed her suspicion. All the money she had scrimped to spend on Michael's riding lessons; there could have been more for him! Jason had pocketed the extra earnings himself. And she had thought he liked her! She felt tears spring to her eyes, as Liz said, "Matt? I don't understand any of this."

"But Jason does, doesn't he?" Matt fixed an acid look on the younger man, and as Jason continued his silence, Matt made a gesture of disgust. "I suggest you leave, Jason. Carrie won't be needing your kind of help any longer."

"But, Matt dear," Barbara intervened quickly, "do you think you should make those kinds of personal decisions for Cory? She does need a job, after all." She gave a tinkling laugh. "The crafts are sweet, dear, but surely not good enough to make a living for you."

"Stay out of this, Barbara," Matt warned in a low voice.

"What on earth is going *on* ?" Liz demanded.

But Jason shuffled to his feet, and threw Carrie an apologetic glance. "Sorry, kid," he turned away. "It's been fun, I guess."

"I'm sorry to disturb you"—Mrs. Bennett appeared at Matt's side—"but it's Michael. He's having another one of those nightmares. He was sleeping soundly just a while ago, but—"

"I'll go up to him, darling," Barbara rose swiftly, but Mrs. Bennett interrupted.

"Excuse me, Miss Breen, but Michael's crying for Carrie."

Barbara's face darkened in anger, but Carrie moved quickly, glad for a chance to escape the merciless scene at the table. More than anything now, she needed peace, a respite from the hubbub of confusion. Racing up the stairs, she heard the doorbell's sudden peal. Some late guests, perhaps, and just as well that they wouldn't meet her in her present state.

The hall light was just bright enough for Carrie to see that Michael had been weeping. "What's the matter, sweetheart?" she took his small warm body into her arms. "Did the dragon come again tonight?"

"Uh huh," his voice quivered, "and it was all black and shiny—and scary."

Softly she soothed him, uneasily tying in once more the occurence of the nightmares with Barbara's appearance in the home. Carrie knew that he was unconsciously afraid of her, fearful that she would threaten the tenuous link between him and Matt. How often Carrie had tried to build Michael's faith in Matt's unending love for him. But the little boy was still afraid.

Tenderly she caressed him, and as his body grew relaxed and sleepy, she laid him back on the pillow.

149

"Don't forget tomorrow, Michael," she murmured and was rewarded by a drowsy smile. "Won't Matt be surprised when he sees you in the horse show? And think about this too, honey. This party means a lot to your brother, and to his business success. We don't want to spoil it for him, do we?"

"No," Michael yawned.

"So you go back to sleep and we'll say a prayer about that old dragon. And for Matt," she added.

"Dear Jesus," Michael whispered, "help Matt find You as a friend. Thank You for Carrie telling me about You. And Jesus, thank You for taking away the dragon."

Carrie softly followed him in prayer, for little Micahel and his childlike faith. Oh, that Matt could have it, too. Michael was asleep in no time and Carrie slipped into his adjoining bathroom to splash cool water on her face.

She had not been in here since the day she had taken the hot, steamy, tub bath, and returned to her apartment only to have Matt come shortly thereafter. The memory filled her with an overwhelming urge to weep. Would she ever be able to think of Matt without tears? Quickly she patted her face dry.

She sat with Michael a moment more, making sure he was sleeping soundly, then soberly she ascended the winding staircase. As she passed Matt's lighted office, she saw in surprise that he and Barbara were there. Matt was behind the desk, Barbara facing him, and there was a tense line to her body. Carrie tiptoed toward the front door, but stopped at Matt's clipped tone.

"Carrie, come in here." Slowly she turned and went into the study. Barbara was looking at her, her green eyes gleaming with a sort of suppressed triumph. Carrie glanced at Matt, puzzled at his expression.

"Carrie," he asked curtly, "what were you saying to Michael upstairs just now?"

"Just now?" she frowned, trying to remember. "Why, nothing, really. I was just trying to soothe him."

"She reminded Michael that your business success meant a lot to her, Matt, and that Michael shouldn't do anything to spoil it." Barbara flashed Carrie a withering look. "I was standing outside the door, and that's exactly what she said."

"Why, no I didn't!" Carrie began. "You've put the wrong interpretation on it."

"On the contrary," Barbara interrupted her, fuming. " *Matt* has the wrong interpretation. I've been telling him all along that you are nothing but a little fortune-hunter, trying to worm your way into this house through Michael. And now here's the proof he needs, as if what he has in his hand isn't enough."

"Quiet, Barbara," Matt interjected firmly, but Carrie saw the disillusionment struggle across his features, and her heart sank.

"What's in your hand, Matt?" she asked.

"It's a bill from the riding stable, just delivered," Barbara informed her triumphantly. "There are an extra twenty lessons on it, all charged to time you used."

Carrie's head reeled. Surely Matt didn't think . . . She could easily straighten out the mistake if she phoned Pete and verified that the hours had been Michael's, and she had paid for them, though apparently not before the bill had been sent. But if she did that, Matt would discover that Michael could ride, and tomorrow's surprise would be ruined for both of them.

". . . flaunting her so-called poverty in front of you, trying to make you feel guilty," Barbara was continuing furiously, "when all along, behind your back, she was using you."

"Carrie," Matt was obviously trying to give her the benefit of the doubt, "this just doesn't sound like you. I would have been happy to let you ride Thunder or any horse—"

"But to go behind his back this way," Barbara pressed on, "well, it's disgusting, and not the first time either, is it, Matt?"

"What was the other time?" Carrie's voice came from a distance. She had seen anger and coldness on Matt's face many times, but this disillusioned expression, as if she had somehow shamed him, hurt more than she could bear.

"Never mind. It's over now," Matt answered curtly, but Barbara wouldn't let it go. Like a hound ferreting out a frightened fox, she moved in for the kill. "Tell her, Matt." she demanded, and Matt swung suddenly to Carrie.

"I knew you were up against it when you arrived here," he said tightly, "and I would have helped you out, if you had asked. But when you pocketed the fine money the magistrate returned to you that morning in court—well, I was surprised, and I mentioned it to Barbara."

"The fine money!" Carrie stared at him, shocked. "Matt, I put that fifty dollars on your desk the very day it was given back to me. You were in California, and I made sure it was set where you would see it the moment you returned."

"A likely story," Barbara sneered.

Carrie looked at Matt, seeing his eyes narrowed in thought, and her heart sank. He would never believe her. So often he had judged her solely on appearance, and he was probably ready to do so again. She lifted her chin. Perhaps it was better this way, the smooth clean break between them that she hadn't been able to make.

"Have you anything else to say, Carrie?" His question cut the air.

"Believe what you will." She turned and walked out of the room, almost colliding with Liz.

"Carrie, I'd like to talk with you," Liz began, but as she noticed Carrie's white face, the huge anguished eyes, she stepped aside. "Perhaps tomorrow at the fair?" she suggested tactfully.

"Tomorrow." Carrie choked on the word, rushing past her.

It was not until she reached the apartment that she let the tears come, sobs that filled her with a sorrow that was just a taste of what the future would bring.

It took her a long time, and the last sounds of the party had finally faded, before her station wagon was packed and ready for the journey home. And Matt never came to her door.

CHAPTER 11

SHE FELT THE TIGHT MISERY in her throat even before she opened her eyes. She had slept fitfully, half of her listening for the familiar tread on the stair, hoping that the party had been only a nightmare. But there was no escaping the facts, she realized, as she sat up and pushed the sleep from her eyes. Jason had betrayed her trust, and worse—much worse—Matt now thought she was a thief.

If he had listened to his instincts, and believed in her. . . But no. She remembered his words, "It isn't wise to get too close to other people." The aloof world he had chosen for himself left him few options.

And she had no options either. Tonight she would turn her station wagon away from Pine Tree Lane, and return to the little home she never should have left. From there she would write Jason and let him know she was quitting her job. If only she had not promised Michael she would attend the fair. How she dreaded the thought of coming face to face with Matt again. She had no desire to look into the beloved gray eyes, eyes that would hold only contempt for her now.

Dressing quickly, she headed for the road, planning to walk to the fairgrounds since her packed car would have to stay hidden until nightfall. But several of the party guests had stayed overnight at Matt's house in order to attend the fair together, and she hadn't gotten very far before a car honked behind her.

"Hop in!" It was Larry's cheerful call, and she slid gratefully into the front seat next to Liz.

"I'm sorry about last night," Liz told her immediately. "I had no idea I was opening a Pandora's box when I admired Jason's merchandise. I certainly don't blame you, Carrie, for leaving early."

"It doesn't matter," Carrie said, glad that Liz didn't know the real reason she had fled Matt's house in disgrace. "Actually, I had begun to suspect something of the sort. It was just so humiliating."

"Never mind. Today you'll see just how saleable your crafts really are."

Carrie threw her a grateful glance, noticing that Liz looked tense, a bit distraught despite her kind words. The scene she had inadvertantly started must have embarrassed her more than she wanted to admit.

Carrie longed to ask her if Matt's engagement was now public knowledge but somehow the words stuck in her throat. "Is. . .is everything settled now between Matt and Barbara?" she finally queried.

Liz shot her a peculiar glance. "I would imagine so," she mused. "And, it's certainly been a long time coming!"

It certainly had, Carrie reflected bitterly. How long had Barbara hung on, waiting for the day when

Michael would accept her? Well, she had her man now, and a dear little boy, too. If only she could make both of them as happy as they deserved to be.

They reached the fairgrounds, and visitors were already mingling among the booths, waiting in line for a turn on the ferris wheel or merry-go-round. Carrie heard the hair-raising screams of those riding the roller coaster, and her pulse quickened. She had always loved the atmosphere of a county fair, and she would try to enjoy this one, too, despite the leaden weight in her heart.

Liz led her to one of the tent-like structures, covered with canvas but open on all sides. Carrie saw a multitude of tables, each displaying a particular specialty.

"Homemade jellies, jams, bread and cakes," Liz murmured as they moved through. "I'd better stay away from those or it's five more pounds on my hips for sure! Let's see, knitted items, personally designed clothes—you should have entered that too, Carrie. Oh, here we are."

It was the art tent, comprised mostly of painting, wall hangings and metal sculpture, but the women threaded their way through the displays until they reached a long table, set against the wall, covered with a pale blue cloth. On it, Carrie recognized her own things. Each piece had been set carefully in a particular place, and the display somehow held a feeling of tenderness, showing her small crafts beautifully. Delicate bowls of blue, white, and golden flowers were scattered among the items, emphasizing their fragile simplicity.

"How incredibly lovely," Carrie sighed.

"I'm glad you like it," Liz smiled. "Matt certainly has the touch, doesn't he?"

"Matt?" Carrie was astonished. "Did he design this table?"

"Of course." Liz looked at her closely. "Haven't you realized yet how much Matt . . ." She stopped, then picked up the conversation briskly. "His idea was to leave your things unpriced, sell them at what people decide to pay. It's a little unorthodox, Carrie, but Matt thinks you ought to discover the value of your own work."

"He's gone to so much trouble." Carrie murmured, but she had no time to mull it over, for as she seated herself behind the table, a customer immediately pounced, lifting several items in admiration.

"Look at this one, Harry," she beckoned to her husband. "What a darling little straw doll and feather broom. And look at the tiny piece of gingham on her skirt." She eyed Carrie with respect. "You made this yourself?"

Carrie nodded, and saw Liz move away, a grin on her face.

"I'll take it," the woman said, "but I can't find a price tag."

"It's . . . whatever you think it's worth," Carrie told her.

"Really?" The woman stared again at the wooden plaque and a smile flitted across her face. "Frankly, dear, I think it's worth more than I can afford. But I'll offer you twenty dollars for it."

"Twenty—" she caught hold of herself. "That would be fine, ma'am. Thank you."

Matt had thoughtfully provided blue-checked paper bags and matching blue ribbon and Carrie deftly wrapped the attactive package for the customer, and sat back to reflect.

Did she really have the kind of talent that could be developed, enlarged? Whatever lay ahead of her, she would always be grateful to Matt for giving her this opportunity. Her once-sagging confidence was beginning to stir again.

The hours flew by. Carrie did a brisk business, as word of mouth brought buyers flocking to her booth. At one point as she glanced up, she caught sight of Matt leaning against one of the outside tent poles, watching her over the heads of the crowd. His eyes were grave, the set of his mouth firm, but Carrie saw a touch of pride in his face and longed to include him in her happiness. But when their eyes met, he turned abruptly and melted into the crowd.

Michael visited her sometime later, cotton candy bits sticking to his cheeks. "The horse show is at six, right after dinner," he whispered, although no eavesdroppers were present.

"I wouldn't miss it for the world," Carrie assured him. "I'm going to have dinner with Liz, then we'll both come and watch."

"Good," Michael declared. "And don't forget to see the touch football game. Matt's signed up to play on the Chicago Bears."

Carrie had seen the announcement, and the thought of watching Matt play football had been flitting through her mind all afternoon.

"I—I don't know, Michael," she murmured, but he had bounded off to the ferris wheel.

By four o'clock Carrie closed her booth. Not only had the customers purchased everything, but she had also taken orders for merchandise to be sent later. Carefully tucking the small fortune into her purse, she walked across the fairgrounds, passing the corral where the horses were grazing, ready for the riding competition. Thunder was there, she noticed, and reminded herself to visit him one last time before she left.

She saw Matt immediately, the broad shoulders filling out his black jersey, and an ache shot through her. Shakily, she sat on the end of the crowded bench, drinking in his rugged appearance, as the pretend Chicago Bears jogged onto the field, to the good-natured hoots of the crowd.

The game was exciting, but Carrie had eyes only for Matt. Despite his large frame, she noticed, he ran like a deer, dodging the opponents with skill and grace. At one point he leaped and caught a pass, crashed into two enormously large men, flipped over their shoulders and skidded into the end zone, bringing a roar of approval from the crowd.

"That's Matt Braden," a man on Carrie's left stated to his companion. "He almost made All-American several years ago, except his knees were so bad."

Sighing wistfully she got up and joined a line for box suppers, and wandered over to the picnic bench where she was to meet Liz. She hadn't yet arrived, and as Carrie sat down, she spotted Matt and Barbara moving through the crowd. They were deep in conversation, and Matt looked angry.

"You love him a great deal, don't you?" Liz's quiet voice reached her, and she turned, unable to hide the bright tears in her eyes.

"I didn't realize it showed that much, Liz," she admitted. "How did you know?"

"I know a great deal about you, little Carrie," Liz said. She was sitting on the picnic bench, and there was a tremor of something indefinable in her voice.

Without speaking, she pulled aside the collar of her blouse, and gently took out a heart locket. Carrie stared at it. It was small and silver. And it had been her mother's.

"Beth?" she whispered, and in a split second Liz's arms had enfolded her and the two of them were weeping together, holding each other as if they would never let go.

Finally Liz pulled away, dabbing at her eyes, and with a shaky smile, pushed Carrie onto the bench. "Sit, little sister," she commanded gently. "You and I have a lot of years to catch up on."

"I don't understand," Carrie shook her head, joy and confusion mingling. "You're really Beth?"

"Elizabeth," Liz reminded her. "Elizabeth Anderson Fields. I changed my nickname when I arrived in Chicago."

"And you've known all this time that I was your sister?" Carrie asked, incredulous. "Ever since the first day we met?"

"Not then," Liz corrected her. "When Larry asked you what your last name was that first day at Woodfield—remember? And you called across the crowd, 'Carrie Craig.' The words just pierced me. I spent two or three sleepless nights pacing the floor, trying to convince myself that there must be hundreds of Carolyn Craigs in the world, and it was just a coincidence that I would meet one who was blond, blue-eyed, and petite like my half-sister had been."

"I didn't even know you heard me that day," Carrie remembered the scene. "It was noisy, and you had turned away."

"Oh, I heard you," Liz chuckled, "and the mystery almost drove me out of my mind. Finally Larry suggested we phone Matt and ask him what he knew. When he pieced together your background for us, we all realized that you had to be my sister."

"Matt knew?" Disappointment flashed through her. "And he never told me. He let me go on making those ridiculous phone calls, making a complete fool out of myself." She bit her lip, but Liz put a consoling hand on her arm.

"Don't blame Matt," she urged. "He's been a loyal friend, and the only person other than Larry who knows all there is to know about me. He wasn't at liberty to discuss me with you, not without violating a very special trust, and he wouldn't do that, not without my permission. But when he told us how you were living, sacrificing so much just to pay a huge telephone bill each month, and when I discovered that somehow you thought I had never cared about you, well, I couldn't remain silent any longer."

"I sensed somehow that you seemed nervous when we would meet occasionally," Carrie said slowly, "But I never dreamed . . . ."

"I *was* nervous," Liz said, smiling. "I was afraid you were going to ask me if I had known your sister, and I didn't think I could look you in the eye and lie to you. You see, Carrie, I didn't think I ought to let you know right away. Matt's reticence was at my insistence. I wanted to get to know you for awhile, to see how you had turned out." She gave Carrie a tremulous, glowing smile. "You've turned out very well.

"But more than that," she hesitated, 'there was an episode in my past, something that might turn you against me if I revealed myself to you."

Carrie nodded slowly. So that was why Matt had warned her off Liz's trail at the restaurant that night.

161

"I don't care what's happened, Liz. All I need to know is why you left."

Liz gazed into the distance, her eyes thoughtful. "For the most obvious reason, Carrie. I'm surprised you haven't considered it already, or perhaps you have. I was sixteen, my parents were dead, and I was pregnant."

"Pregnant? And you weren't . . ."

"Married? No." Liz smiled slightly. "He was nothing more than an acquaintance, really. I can't even remember his face now." She turned back to Carrie, and her expression was a mixture of shame and defensiveness. "I'll tell you how it all happened, that is, if you still want to listen."

"Liz," Carrie told her firmly, "I loved you even before I discovered you were Beth. I want to know everything, if you want to tell me."

It was the sort of story one reads in a magazine, Carrie marveled, half of her hanging on every word, the other half longing to reach out and comfort Liz as she unfolded the tale. Liz had apparently felt rejected when her mother married Carrie's father, as if the couple's happiness was so total that there was no room left for her. And when Carrie was born, the feeling grew deeper. "I know now that there was no basis for it," Liz explained, "but at the time—well, I was young and impetuous."

Rebelling one evening, she allowed a boy from school to take her to a motel room, and shortly after, discovered she was pregnant. Before she could tell her parents, they were killed, and in order not to be a burden to Gramps, who now had Carrie to rear, she left immediately after the funeral.

"I went to a home for unwed mothers in Chicago,

162

registered under another name, and finished high school through a correspondence course," she explained. "The baby, a boy, was adopted right after birth. Of course, I have no idea where he is now."

"Oh, Liz, that must have been so hard."

"Hard, yes, but right, Carrie. I would have had no home to offer him. Anyway, I stayed in Chicago, went to college at night, began working for a big department store and, well, you know the rest."

"Not really." Carrie looked at her. "Why didn't you ever come back to us?"

"Ah, Carrie," Liz sighed, "that's the hardest part to explain." She shook her head slowly. "You and Gramps, there was a sort of chemistry between you, something that I could never share. I would have been an outsider. And how could I have explained the situation? You know how the neighbors would have talked: an out-of-wedlock pregnancy in a nice Christian home. And Gramps was quite firm about his standards of morality. He raised you well. But how do you think he would have felt about me?"

Carrie nodded again, recognizing the truth in Liz's words. Gramps had been a purist in his approach to life, and as much as he believed the Bible, forgiveness for such an action would have been almost impossible for him.

"There were things I didn't know, however," Liz went on. "For one, I never realized that you would remember me, much less miss me. You were so young when I left. I loved you very much, but I thought I would eventually recede into the back of your mind, especially if I made certain never to correspond with you."

"But you did," Carrie reminded her quickly. "That

last note, four years ago, was what led me to Woodfield in the first place."

"That was Larry's idea," Liz answered. "We had just been married, and he felt strongly that I should let Gramps know that I was happily settled in life. I guess I felt a stab of conscience and wanted to reassure him.

"And then," she went on more easily now, as if the words, pent up for so long, were rushing to be freed. "I also didn't know what a hard time the two of you were having financially, with just Gramps' government pension. I'd assumed that our folks left some insurance in addition to the house."

"They didn't," Carrie said, "but we got along fine, Liz, really we did. Don't punish yourself because of me."

"I'll regret that to my dying day," Liz murmured. "I could have sent you both money from time to time if I had known. If it's any consolation to you at this late date, Carrie, I've written to the town's lawyer, clearing any claim I have to the property. It's all yours, now, if you should ever want to sell it."

"Well, I guess I won't be selling it," Carrie looked at the ground, fighting a sudden urge to weep. "I— I'm going back, Liz. Tonight."

"Tonight! But you can't." Alarmed, Liz grasped her hand. "Carrie, we've only just found each other; we've years to catch up on."

"I know," she swallowed hard, "but—"

"It's Matt, isn't it?" Liz's tone held a gentle understanding at the misery on Carrie's face. "Carrie, look. Matt respected my trust and I have to respect his as well. But you don't understand everything yet. There's more here than meets the eye. Stay and see it through, won't you?"

"I can't," Carrie turned imploringly to Liz. "Please understand. I'm so grateful and glad that we found each other, and we will share a great deal of time together someday. You've no idea how I've dreamed of it. But right now," she swallowed against the rising lump in her throat. "seeing Matt is too painful for me, and I have to get away for awhile."

"I understand," Liz slipped a consoling arm around her. "But I wish you'd wait, Carrie. You're judging only on what you see, and that's not the whole picture."

Judging with her eyes and not with her heart? How often she had accused Matt of doing that to her! But she had to leave. She was a thief in his eyes now, and there was no way to undo the past.

She sighed. "I'm not hungry, Liz. Would you mind if we walked over to the corral? The beginner class should be starting soon and I promised Michael I'd be there. I want to see him one last time before I go."

"You always were stubborn, Carrie, even when you were little." But Liz's eyes were soft. "Sure, I'll go. I wouldn't want to miss Michael's big moment either."

It wasn't Michael that Carrie sought as they neared the corral, however. Worried, her eyes swung from face to face. Where was Matt? What if he missed Michael's performance after all these weeks of practice?

"There he is," Liz nodded. "Up in the grandstand, sitting with the Hardings."

"Oh, yes." Carrie's legs went limp as she saw Matt with a couple from the party last night. The familiar curt line etched his jaw, and his eyes searched the crowd, apparently looking for someone.

"He looks mad," Liz mused. "I wonder where Barbara went?"

"I'm sure they'll find each other," Carrie murmured. There was no point in telling Liz about the ugly scene in Matt's office, about whom his anger was really directed toward.

Fortunately, the master of ceremonies had come to the center of the ring with a list of competing riders, and she watched Matt's swift, almost disinterested gaze scan the corral. Then Michael's name was announced, and his head turned in stunned disbelief.

Pride ran through Carrie as Michael rode into the ring, perched astride Rosie with the calm, easy grace of a veteran horseman. His eyes darted around the corral, and as he caught sight of her, he threw her a triumphant smile.

"Oh, Carrie," Liz murmured next to her, "You've done so much with Michael. And look at Matt. He's positively bursting."

She did, fastening her longing eyes on him for the last time, glad that she would remember the expression of love and pride now revealed on his face as he watched Michael.

Throughout the event, the young boy maintained a natural poise and a genuine smile. And at the end, when the riders were lined across the ring, and the judge handed him a third-place ribbon, Carrie thought she would burst with joy. But her smile was short-lived.

"I have to go, Liz," she murmured, a deep shudder tearing through her. "I want to stop at the pasture and say goodbye to Thunder, and then I'll be on my way."

Liz went with her, silent, and as they approached the paddock fence they were both astonished to see

Barbara coming toward them. Carrie stiffened at the sight of her and would have turned away, but Liz put a firm arm around her.

"What are you doing here, Barbara?" she queried.

"Actually, I was coming to look for Cory. This poor brute," she indicated Thunder, "is going absolutely crazy for some exercise. Pete brought him over with the others, thinking that Matt would be riding today, but he isn't, and Thunder's getting terribly anxious being so cooped up."

"Then why don't you ride him yourself?" Liz suggested.

"I haven't got the touch," Barbara admitted. Her green eyes swept across Carrie, glittering with a peculiar sort of malice. "Cory's the only woman who can handle him. You proved that once, didn't you, dear?"

Choosing not to respond, Carrie instead fastened her eyes on Thunder. He did look nervous, dancing impatiently, and she remembered the glorious day they had sailed over the hurdles together.

"So, I thought," Barbara suddenly gushed, "that *you* might ride him, dear. Just to run a little spirit out of him?"

"Oh, I couldn't," Carrie said swiftly. "He belongs to Matt." But the longing to be in Thunder's saddle once more was evident in her eyes because Liz turned to her with pleasure.

"Go ahead, Carrie," she urged. "I know Matt wouldn't mind. And besides, I've never seen you ride, and I'd like to, very much."

There was a poignant note in Liz's voice, a reminder of the years they had lost, and Carrie succumbed. "Just for you, Liz," she agreed.

"Wonderful. I'll shorten the stirrups for you, dear." Barbara went around to Thunder's other side and Carrie thought it strange that the stallion was already bridled and saddled. Apparently Barbara had done that, too. *She must care about Thunder more than I realized,* Carrie thought. A perplexed frown flitted across her brow at Barbara's suddenly pleasant behavior, but she could spare no time to wonder about it. For as she approached, Thunder nickered in recognition, and a wave of excitement swept over her.

"Just one last time, boy," she murmured, swinging herself into the saddle. "A ride to last me forever."

Quickly she headed Thunder for the fenced-in pasture just beyond the corral. It was a show-jumping ring, but there was plenty of room for an easy canter. She touched him lightly and spoke the command softly. Thunder broke smoothly into a canter, his mane flying, and she could feel his pent-up power, eager to be released. A surge of joy shot through her once again. He was a noble animal, superb, and aching for a good run as much as he was, Carrie nonetheless held him in check. They rounded a turn, and just ahead of them loomed the lower competition hurdles. Her mind raced at the sight. Could she take Thunder over one of them?

Past all vestiges of common sense she headed him for the nearest jump. "Go, boy!" she whispered, and the horse's ears flickered in understanding. His powerful body responded to her touch and as they approached the bar, Carrie eased forward in the saddle, anticipating the grandeur of the leap.

And then it was as if an explosion had blown her from the saddle. Thunder shied, rammed into the side rails, and fell heavily to the ground, sending Carrie skidding sideways along the rough grass. Bruised and dazed she pulled herself to her feet, staggering in panic back to where Thunder still lay, struggling to stand.

"Oh, Thunder," she cried, anguished beyond belief. "Thunder, please get up. Dear God, please help him."

Eyes blurred with mist she saw that Liz was racing toward her, followed by others. "Carrie!" she screamed, "are you all right?"

"It's Thunder," she whispered. "Why doesn't he get up?" Carrie shook her head in disbelief as the horse would roll up on his side only to jerk at some unknown pain and fall back. A shocked trembling started in her legs, spreading throughout her body. "He was heading for the hurdles, and then . . ." But he hadn't been trained for jumps! Matt had told her once.

She looked up, her eyes caught sight of a man running with a slight limp across the pasture.

"Oh, Liz," Carrie said, wildly, "It's Matt, and I can't face him. I've ruined everything."

"Carrie, don't go." Liz reached a sympathetic hand out to her, but she wheeled in the other direction, frantically attempting to out-run the unbearable pain that had wrapped itself around her. "Oh, Matt, how you must hate me," she sobbed, stumbling in her haste to reach her packed car and drive away forever. But the picture of Matt bending over the straining animal, as he must surely be doing at this moment, was one that would torment her the rest of her life.

CHAPTER 12

IT WAS DUSK BEFORE CARRIE had finally skirted Chicago, and found herself on the open road. The congestion had taken a toll on her overwrought nerves, and despite her need for haste she pulled off the highway for a moment to collect herself. She would need calm nerves to drive through this terrible traffic, especially if she continued through the night.

She rested for a moment, her head tilted against the seat, and the unbidden thought of Matt crept across her heart. She would need the healing powers of time and prayer to smoothe away the jagged edges of her pain, quiet the part of her that threatened to break loose in a spasm of torment. His beloved face, shocked at what her stupidity had done to Thunder . . .

Dear God, she said inwardly, *I've prayed that You could change Matt's heart, that He would know You and love You, and ask You to rule his life. I'm sorry that I acted so foolishly. I've probably turned his heart to stone forever. But please, someday, help him to forgive me.*

She had not traveled much farther, and night had barely fallen on the surrounding corn fields, when a red light illuminated her dashboard. There was trouble of some kind under the hood, and Carrie knew from bitter experience that if she did not have it looked at right away, the battered old car would balk, and she would be stranded. Hastily she turned off the highway, and located a service station.

The attendant cheerfully found the trouble, a shortage of water in the engine's radiator, but as she set down the container, he frowned.

"That engine's overheating badly, even with the water. If I were you, I'd give it several hours rest before starting out again, especially if you're going far."

Carrie thought. Even at the wagon's slow bumpy pace, she had planned on arriving home well before dawn. But she knew enough to follow the attendant's advice.

"Is there a motel nearby?" she asked, and he directed her to one a few blocks away.

She checked into the motel, using the money from the sale of her crafts that day at the fair. And later, as she lay in the quiet darkness of the room, she wondered what Matt's reaction would be when he found the envelope she had left on his desk stuffed with most of her profits. He had once told her seriously that a lease was a legal contract, and since she was breaking hers, it was only right that he should be paid the remaining rent.

She had thought to add a note, something to express her sorrow over Thunder, but when the time came, she had been without words. How could she capture in a shaky scrawl the depths of her anguish, and how much Matt had meant—would always mean—to her?

Impatiently she wadded up her pillow and pressed her face against it, hoping sleep would come.

The next day was a glorious summer morning, and under normal circumstances Carrie would have relished the sight of the fertile fields, bursting and ready for next month's harvest. But she saw them as though she were looking through a veil.

She glanced automatically at the on-coming traffic, gauging its pace, hugging the right-hand side of the road in her usual desperate fashion. But now, surveying the road, she saw to her astonishment that a red Mercedes-Benz was zipping along the highway, moving smartly in and out of the traffic. It couldn't be. But as the sports car whizzed by her on the opposite side of the road, there was no doubt in her mind. It had been Matt.

Had he seen her? What was he doing on the highway, coming from the other direction?

Panic flooded her. Quickly she pulled off the highway at the first exit and sped down the country road, sided by peaceful paddocks. She would hide here until she was sure he had not seen her and doubled back.

Alighting from the car, she went over to the fence, pressing her flushed face against the hard comfort of the wooden stakes. A small mare, grazing in the center of the field, pricked up her ears, stared at Carrie, and trotted over, followed by her little foal.

"Hello, you beauties." Carrie rubbed her fingers against the suedy texture of their muzzles, inhaling the familiar heady aroma of horseflesh. "Wish I had an apple for each of you."

The mare pressed her soft nose into Carrie's outstretched hand, and she rubbed her cheek against the daintily arched neck. The little horse reminded her painfully of Rosie, and Rosie reminded her of Thunder, and Thunder reminded her . . . "Stop it!" she scolded herself.

And just then she heard the slam of a car door. The red Mercedes was standing by the road, and Matt walked toward her. She sensed his anger and, alarmed, she turned to the fence. If she could climb over. . .But his firm hand was on her arm. "Matt, let me go!" Her voice rose in panic.

Instead he pulled her around to him.

"Matt, don't!" She tried to struggle free, but he picked her up easily and carried her to his car, dropping her unceremoniously on the front seat and sliding in beside her.

"Matt, please!" She turned to him, her voice shaking, and all of a sudden the terror left her. This was Matt, the man she loved! She knew he could be reasonable when it suited him, and he had promised never to hurt her again. Why had she been afraid?

Or was it herself that she feared, her own crumbling defense that would betray her true feelings in a minute if she did not hold herself together?

She glanced at him out of the corner of her eye, and noticed that he had made no move to start the engine. Instead, with unsteady hands he lit a cigarette—only the second time she had seen him smoke—and fastened his eyes on something in the distance. His profile was an inscrutable mask. Minutes passed, and finally his taut voice broke the silence.

"I've been driving all night," he said, "and I'm a little edgy now from lack of sleep."

She saw the tired lines around his eyes. "Driving all night?"

"I had been looking for you at the fair, and when Liz told me you had gone right after the fall, I left immediately," he explained in that same flat tone. "I reached your home town during the wee hours this morning. Your house was vacant and no one had seen you, so I came back by another route. Fortunately, I spotted you on the highway just now." He turned for a moment. "You do know about Liz now, don't you?"

"Yes," she nodded quietly. "I understand everything, and she's wonderful. And I'm grateful to you for the part you played in it all."

"Yet you still feel it's necessary to run away?"

"Matt, I have to," she protested. "Why did you follow me?"

"Because we're going to talk now, Carrie," he told her firmly. "We're going to talk the way we never have before, with complete honesty, no holds barred. We should have done it long before this. In fact, I was planning to the night of the party."

"But you never came." Her voice echoed the wound within her.

"There were other things to consider then."

"I can imagine." How much additional venom had Barbara flung after Carrie's exit from the office?

He spoke softly now. "When we've finished with this conversation, if you still want to go home, I promise I won't stand in your way. Agreed?"

She swallowed hard. She didn't *want* to go home! Seeing Matt had torn apart her resolve, dashed it into

174

a million pieces. Could she be completely honest, and still walk away from him when everything was over?

"All right," she murmured, and saw him relax slightly.

"First of all," he began, "I have a broken-hearted little boy on my hands right now. I want to hear it from your own lips. I want you to tell me straight out that you don't care about Michael any more."

"That's not fair," she protested. "I love Michael, more than you'll ever know. I tried to tell him that in the letter I left for him, but—"

"Oh yes, your letter. Should I tell Michael to put it under his pillow at night? Will it take away his nightmares, his heartaches? Did Liz's letter take away yours?"

She put her trembling hands to her ears, but with one swift motion he mashed his cigarette in the ash tray and reached up both his hands to grasp her wrists and hold them down.

"How can you leave him, Carrie? He needs you."

"I know he needs me," she cried out. "But there isn't a place for me in his life. Can't you understand, Matt? I would feel like a pawn being moved around to suit everyone but myself."

He dropped her hands suddenly, and when he spoke again, his voice was resigned. "I did treat you like a pawn, didn't I, Carrie? You asked once why I practically forced you into my life, but you had already guessed the answer. It was for Michael's sake, at least at first. I saw his eyes light up with a sort of inner happiness that I hadn't been able to give him. And even though you reminded me of a miserable time in my own life, I had to make certain that you stayed, at least for awhile."

"And so you bribed me?"

"At first," he admitted. Carrie noticed the dampness on his forehead and realized that, despite his cool exterior, Matt was fighting an inner duel with himself, finding it painfully difficult to expose his thoughts.

"And then," he began again, and there was a touch of wonder to his words. "And then, something began to happen. I don't know how you did it, but you managed to bring a sense of joy into all our lives. The little flowers you planted, your laughter, your whole way of life, so foreign to my own. Everywhere I looked, you had left the imprint of yourself. I began to care about you, Carrie." His voice softened. "Not only because of what you were doing for Michael, but because of what you were doing for me. I saw something very special in you, Carrie. Even when your temper wanted to get the best of you, there was a strength that seemed to control you. You have a faith that guides every part of your life. I want to know your God—that God who is so dear to you, who is so dear to Michael."

The words hung between them like a shining star, glowing and beautiful, and Carrie felt a rush of joy. God had answered her prayer!

"I tried to let you know how I felt that night in the restaurant," he went on. "I wanted to make it the beginning of something, but you're so young, I was afraid you would think I was only trying to take advantage of you." He sat quietly for a moment. "Can't we make a fresh start, Carrie? Can't you come back?"

"But, Matt," she said, searching for more words. Didn't he know what he was asking? How could she

176

stand by, a fifth wheel, an outsider in their family circle, pretending friendship while suffering from an unreturned love? "You and Barbara—"

"Barbara!" He spoke with disgust. "She's behind all of this, isn't she?"

"Well, of course she is," Carrie began, but he cut her off with an irritated gesture and then sighed, leaning his arms against the steering wheel again. "Then," he muttered, "I suppose you'll have to hear it all before you understand."

"I don't want to know any more," she began.

"Well, you're going to listen," he said, and continued to speak.

"During my last few years in college," he explained slowly, "I went through a sort of rebellion. I suppose a lot of anger was bottled up inside me, and I took part in a lot of foolish pranks, one of them, unfortunately, on the dean. He was so furious when he found out I was behind it I was lucky not to be expelled. But, I lost his respect, and it cost me a good deal more. After graduation I learned for the first time the value of a good reputation. My grades had been excellent, I was a well-known athlete, but because I had been such a troublemaker, especially with that last episode, the dean saw to it that not one of my professors would recommend me for a job."

He paused, and Carrie drew in her breath. She thought *she* had known hardship and rejection! How had it been for him—a bright and talented man who had made almost as many wrong choices as she had.

"By that time my back was against the wall, financially," Matt continued. "I couldn't play professional ball because of my knees, Michael was on the way, and my father was sick and needed care. I was

177

the only one the family could depend on. It was then that I met Barbara. She persuaded her boss to take a chance on me despite my reckless background, and because of that, I got my start.''

''I see.'' She could understand now his gratitude to Barbara.

''It was inevitable, I suppose, during those early years, that Barbara and I should drift into a relationship,'' he went on. ''Gradually, however, she demanded more of me than I was willing to give, so a few years ago we made a clean break. She still acted as my hostess, stayed in the guest room when we flew out early in the morning, but as far as any closeness goes . . .'' He shrugged.

''But you're going to marry her,'' Carrie burst out. ''How can you say there's no closeness when—''

''Marry her? Who gave you that idea?''

''Why, she did.''

''I get it now,'' he said slowly. ''So she filled you full of lies, too.''

''What do you mean?'' Carrie whispered.

''I forced the truth out of her after the party, most of it, that is. Before I saw Michael in the show, and realized the meaning of that riding bill, I knew something just wasn't right. You're too trusting, too honest. You even left me that ridiculous packet of rent money.'' He sighed. ''I deliberately exposed Jason to you, just so you could see him for the kind of man he really is. I couldn't face the possibility that you were planning on spending the rest of your life with him.''

''But I never—''

''I know,'' he said. ''Barbara admitted that was a lie too, when we had our final quarrel at the fair. And then, when we found the burr under Thunder's saddle—"

"The burr?" Dread and disbelief mingled in her voice.

"Barbara had placed it so it would prick him just as you leaned forward for a jump. That's why he was slow getting up, too. Whenever he rolled forward it stabbed him again. Once we found the cause, though, he jumped up and was fine. Whether she meant to hurt you or Thunder, or maybe both of you . . ." He sighed.

"Thunder is okay?" Carrie asked in a small voice, and suddenly from deep within her, a sob rose to her lips. And another, and another. Like a tidal wave they enveloped her, and she collapsed against Matt's chest. He gathered her in his arms, his touch gentle, one strong hand stroking her hair. In wrenching sobs, the days of suppressed sorrow poured forth. She clutched him, gasping disjointed phrases as he murmured things she could barely hear.

"She made you believe terrible things about me," Carrie choked.

"Hush," he whispered, his cheek rough against her hair. "Give me credit for some understanding, however late it arrived."

"And the fine money," Carrie gasped, "I didn't . . . I didn't . . ."

Another wave of tears shook her and his arm tightened protectively around her. "Ah, Carrie," he murmured, a terrible regret in his voice, "I know. I've hurt you so much when all I ever wanted to do was hold you, and care for you, and love you for the rest of my life."

"Love me?" she quavered, the warmth of his words penetrating her thoughts.

"Love you," he said firmly, and she heard the rough edge to his voice. "And now you know, now that I've driven you away with my anger, my blindness. . . ."

"Oh, no." She sat up and looked at him. Slowly she reached out her fingertips and traced the beloved profile, then turned his disbelieving face to hers. "I love you, Matt," she whispered. "I always have."

She saw the fire of joy leap into his eyes before he seized her and pulled her toward him. "Carrie, my beloved."

Slowly he covered her damp face with his kisses, and she moved closer into the circle of his arms. Then he gently lifted his head and looked down at her, his gray eyes aglow with a silver flame. Reaching into his back pocket, he handed Carrie a small box. "It's not a ring—we'll get one today—but I thought you might like to have it. I showed it to Liz last week."

Liz. No wonder her sister had warned her that she didn't fully understand the situation. Inside the box was the small, silver heart locket they had seen in the store window. He had even had it engraved. "Carrie" and "Matt" the two sides proclaimed.

"I'm not much with words," Matt was saying, "but I thought when I gave it to you, you might understand how I felt. But I never got the chance, not until now."

"Oh, Matt." She felt another rush of tears, tears of overwhelming love for his thoughtfulness. "You did this for me?"

"That's just the beginning," he said. "Would you like to go on the Paris trip with me, as a sort of honeymoon? We could stay on for awhile, send for Michael and Mrs. Bennett when school starts, and you could study art."

"Paris?" she gasped, awed. "But what about your house, your job?"

"The house?" he shrugged. "I could rent it out temporarily, let someone else enjoy it until we fill it with our own children. And the job . . ." She caught a hint of uncertainty behind his words. "How would you feel if I followed that star you once told me about?"

She reached up to his forehead, smoothing the urgent look away. "Michael said it once, better than I ever could," she told him, and the promise of a lifetime of faith rested in her words. "Paris, Colorado, or a tent in the middle of nowhere. I don't care where I live, Matt, as long as you're there."

He reached gently for her chin, turning her loving face toward his, and met her lips in the language they now shared, the language of the heart.

ABOUT THE AUTHOR

JEANNE ANDERS has authored five books on subjects of interest to the family, in addition to writing hundreds of magazine articles, and columns for various publications. Lest you think she is a lady of leisure with nothing but time for dipping her pen into the inkwell, you should also know that Jeanne is a busy wife and mother of five children, is involved with a Bible study and prayer group, and lectures to women's clubs on family topics. This is her first inspirational romance novel—a happy addition to her writing talents.

A Letter To Our Readers

Dear Reader:

In order that we might better contribute to your reading enjoyment, we would appreciate your taking a few minutes to respond to the following questions and return to:

Editor, Serenade Books
The Zondervan Publishing House
1415 Lake Drive, S.E.
Grand Rapids, Michigan 49506

1. Did you enjoy reading LANGUAGE OF THE HEART?

   ☐ Very much. I would like to see more books by this author!
   ☐ Moderately
   ☐ I would have enjoyed it more if _____

2. Where did you purchase this book? _____

3. What influenced your decision to purchase this book?

   ☐ Cover   ☐ Back cover copy
   ☐ Title   ☐ Friends
   ☐ Publicity   ☐ Other _____

4. Would you be interested in reading other Serenade/Serenata or Serenade/Saga Books?

☐ Very interested
☐ Moderately interested
☐ Not interested

5. Please indicate your age range:

☐ Under 18   ☐ 25–34   ☐ 46–55
☐ 18–24   ☐ 35–45   ☐ Over 55

6. Would you be interested in a Serenade book club? If so, please give us your name and address:

Name _____

Occupation _____

Address _____

City _____ State _____ Zip _____

Serenade Saga books are inspirational romances in historical settings, designed to bring you a joyful, heart-lifting reading experience.

Serenade Saga books available in your local book store:

#1   SUMMER SNOW, Sandy Dengler
#2   CALL HER BLESSED, Jeanette Gilge
#3   INA, Karen Baker Kletzing
#4   JULIANA OF CLOVER HILL,
      Brenda Knight Graham
#5   SONG OF THE NEREIDS, Sandy Dengler
#6   ANNA'S ROCKING CHAIR,
      Elaine Watson
#7   IN LOVE'S OWN TIME,
      Susan C. Feldhake
#8   YANKEE BRIDE, Jane Peart
#9   LIGHT OF MY HEART, Kathleen Karr
#10   LOVE BEYOND SURRENDER,
      Susan C. Feldhake
#11   ALL THE DAYS AFTER SUNDAY,
      Jeannette Gilge
#12   WINTERSPRING, Sandy Dengler
#13   HAND ME DOWN THE DAWN,
      Mary Harwell Sayler
#14   REBEL BRIDE, Jane Peart
#15   SPEAK SOFTLY, LOVE, Kathleen Yapp
#16   FROM THIS DAY FORWARD, Kathleen Karr
#17   THE RIVER BETWEEN, Jacquelyn Cook
#18   VALIANT BRIDE, Jane Peart
#19   WAIT FOR THE SUN, Maryn Langer
#20   KINCAID OF CRIPPLE CREEK, Peggy Darty

#21 LOVE'S GENTLE JOURNEY, Kay Cornelius
#22 APPLEGATE LANDING, Jean Conrad

Serenade Serenata books are inspirational romances in contemporary settings, designed to bring you a joyful, heart-lifting reading experience.

Serenade Serenata books available in your local bookstore:

#1   ON WINGS OF LOVE, Elaine L. Schulte
#2   LOVE'S SWEET PROMISE,
      Susan C. Feldhake
#3   FOR LOVE ALONE, Susan C. Feldhake
#4   LOVE'S LATE SPRING, Lydia Heermann
#5   IN COMES LOVE, Mab Graff Hoover
#6   FOUNTAIN OF LOVE, Velma S. Daniels and
      Peggy E. King.
#7   MORNING SONG, Linda Herring
#8   A MOUNTAIN TO STAND STRONG,
      Peggy Darty
#9   LOVE'S PERFECT IMAGE, Judy Baer
#10 SMOKY MOUNTAIN SUNRISE,
      Yvonne Lehman
#11 GREENGOLD AUTUMN,
      Donna Fletcher Crow
#12 IRRESISTIBLE LOVE, Elaine Anne McAvoy
#13 ETERNAL FLAME, Lurlene McDaniel
#14 WINDSONG, Linda Herring
#15 FOREVER EDEN, Barbara Bennett
#16 CALL OF THE DOVE, Madge Harrah
#17 THE DESIRES OF YOUR HEART,
      Donna Fletcher Crow
#18 TENDER ADVERSARY, Judy Baer
#19 HALFWAY TO HEAVEN, Nancy Johanson

#20 HOLD FAST THE DREAM,
Lurlene McDaniel
#21 THE DISGUISE OF LOVE,
Mary LaPietra
#22 THROUGH A GLASS DARKLY,
Sara Mitchell

Watch for other books in both the *Serenade Saga* (historical) and *Serenade Serenata* (contemporary) series coming soon.